WAKE UP, ALI...
WAKE UP NOW

WAKE UP, ALI... WAKE UP NOW

A SOUTH ASIAN DIASPORIC STORY

Sumit Sharma Sameer

Translated from Nepali by Sushrut Acharya

Vitasta

LET KNOWLEDGE SPREAD

Published by

Renu Kaul Verma
Vitasta Publishing Pvt Ltd
2/15, Ansari Road, Daryaganj
New Delhi - 110 002
info@vitastapublishing.com

ISBN: 978-93-90961-06-1

First Edition 2022

MRP ₹395

This novel is entirely a work of fiction. Names, characters, events and incidents are entirely imaginary. Reference to real places, actual regions, institutions or community practices has been made in a fictitious manner. Any resemblance to actual persons, living or dead or actual events is purely coincidental.

The views, thoughts and opinions expressed in the book belong solely to author, and neither to the author's employer nor to his position of employment.

Edited by Kanagam King
Typeset by TagElements
Cover Design by Somesh Kumar Mishra
Printed by Chaman Enterprises, Delhi

Contents

Search

Have you ever noticed ants running in various directions on a bright sunny day? Have you scrutinized them? Carefully? My mind is sometimes drawn to these wandering ants. I am enchanted by their motion. I wonder – why this restlessness? Such small creatures, yet such great energy!

This energy of theirs excites me. I feel a certain thrumming within me. Their motion compels me to ponder the universe. I wonder – what drives them? Are they terrified of the shadow of their own existence? What do they lust after? Are they moving to external beats, terrorized by sound? Are they powered by the sunlight that falls on them?

I don't know about ants, but one particular notion is getting clearer – my personal life is no different from those crawling insects'. I too had great energy within me. I too ran hither and thither in whatever direction life pulled me. I wasn't aware – was I being led by my desires? Or was I afraid of my own existence? Was fate steering me? Or was I being guided by some invisible divine power?

Those ants have a certain essence. As do I. An ant is a living being. As am I. Like the ants, I lived within my community. But also as an individual. They communicated via pheromones. I took pleasure in inner discourse. Every so often, a voice deep within me would resound again and again – 'Wake up, Ali. You've been asleep a lifetime. Wake up now.'

This voice appeared around the same time as my self-awareness – when I became aware of my own individuality. Sometimes the voice was harsh, and sometimes extremely soft and melodious. Sometimes it was frightening, and at other times calm. I have lived through fifty springs, and all who were intimately connected to me have said their goodbyes. Yet, that voice never let go of me.

Mother passed away when I was twelve; father when I was thirty. I was never close with my relatives. And so called friends, acquired over an expended life, took constant advantage of me; treated me poorly. The effects of these traumas, experienced over various periods, long lingered within me. They diminished me. But they also gave me strength. They made me introverted, yet outgoing. They made me materialistic, but also spiritual. They gave me education, yet also prejudices. My life experiences made me a person who could take pleasure in his own company.

Being alone takes skill. And solitude can be addicting – a sweet intoxication for those who enjoy it; an intoxication that razes down ambition. That is perhaps why, presently, I found the ambitions of my youth comical. I had become frightful of the idea of becoming rich and famous. I felt as if wealth and fame would demand a sacrifice of my very self – as if even my shadow would vanish in search of its own existence!

The things that made up the building blocks of my life were losing energy and urgency. I couldn't tell if I was becoming whole or more dispersed. Was I becoming freer? Or snared in ever newer webs? Was I finding myself, or getting tangled in the complexities of life and death? Life doesn't simply follow a straight line – it isn't conducted merely according to a plan. It is directed by myriad worldly and other-worldly elements. It is irrigated and operated by plans well beyond man's understanding. It is, therefore, always unstable.

Though well fed and imposing, my body housed an unstable Ali. But no one besides me recognized that unstable Ali. The volatility compelled me to live with a fractured psyche all my life. So much so that I am uncertain, to this day, about whether I did the right thing in marrying Zara. As uncertain as I was on the day of our wedding.

It is not easy to live with a fractured psyche. Nor is it happy. Most people don't easily accept this fact. Yet, all are cursed to live like that. 'Why?' I wonder. Perhaps a splintered life is man's fate – his supreme truth. And I too was a victim of my own truth. Therefore, I remained agitated all my life. Sometimes in sentiment; sometimes, in intense passion.

Periodically, that intensity would invite quarrels – with my own wife Zara. We usually fought about the practicalities of the household. She didn't know of my pain – never had I bothered to express myself to her. I hadn't wanted to appear weak, easily overwhelmed by sentiment. Society doesn't grant a man that permission – he must always be fearless and strong. Like an unfeeling cold steel headstone.

Zara was ten years younger than me. Not particularly pretty; but also not one you could call unattractive. Short with large eyes, but missing the usual spark found in such eyes. Aloof and impassive; I can't remember the last time she smiled. It was as if she'd disappeared somewhere; only her body remained near me. I never did try to find the hiding Zara. Our daughter Ayesha was the only one keeping us connected. She was our little princess – the light of our eyes, our delicate flower. Zara and I had started to irritate and annoy each other. Daily quarrels – especially about money – had become the norm.

One day she said, 'Ali, I need five thousand to pay for Ayesha's tutoring.'

'I don't have any money, Zara,' I replied.

'You can't avoid the matter so easily. Do you think I am asking for myself? I take no joy in having to beg in front of you.' She was annoyed.

'Let's not talk about money,' I tried to change the subject. 'Let's talk about something else.'

'What else should we talk about but our present needs? And joy if I were so lucky to find you free to listen to the things I have to say!' Her mockery was always painful.

She further added, 'I don't understand why despite being a civil engineer you earn so less? Look at other civil engineers, they seem to earn so much. It's all my fate.'

'Why do you taunt me so? Whatever I earn, my entire salary, I place in your hands at the end of every month. I don't keep a single cent for myself. How am I going to get more money – steal?'

'O, Allah! He wouldn't hesitate to blame me if he ever turned to crime! You think I am only concerned about money – don't you?' She was angry. 'Yes, you contribute your salary. But it's not enough to cover our household expenses,' she added. 'Everything has become more expensive. Even our combined income barely supports us.'

'Then let's spend a little less,' I promptly suggested. 'We can't go on like this.'

'Spend less? How? Should we not eat? Should we not send our daughter to school? Or observe the festivals? Should we forego medical treatment? Or stop buying Akib's and your medicine? Have you ever seen me buy anything for myself? Have we ever gone anywhere for a vacation?' Her eyes began to tear up.

I didn't have answers to Zara's questions.

'Just the other night, our daughter asked if we could go out on a trip,' she continued. 'She says all her friends go on trips with their parents. Now how do I explain things to the child? But you can't be bothered. Why would you be? After all you hand over your entire salary to me! What – is Ayesha only my responsibility?'

'Careful, Zara! Don't overstep your bounds,' I raised my voice. 'You are accusing me of failing in my responsibilities towards my own daughter.'

'I am only saying that you haven't cared to understand what I am going through. Have you once asked me how I am managing to run the house under such difficult circumstances? What's more – you accuse me of spending irresponsibly. Spewing out whatever comes to mind! Alright, please tell me, what exactly am I supposed to do?' She threw another barb.

'Don't argue with me! Our daughter wasn't born into a wealthy family. She's not entitled to more than what she has. Explain that to her. If you'd done your job properly, you wouldn't have to talk back like that. Even the skin off my back wouldn't be sufficient for these ingrates,' I ranted in rage.

Zara wasn't going to take it lying down. She started shouting. 'I have never met anyone so callous. Skin off your back? How can you even say that? What have you ever done to help the family off its difficulties? It's useless to talk to you. This stupid argument is making me late to work. But keep this in mind – this state of affairs will not do. I am not going to take care of anything from now on. You run your own household.'

'I am not your servant! Don't you dare make demands of me! I don't even have time to look at your face.' My anger knew no bounds. I could not control myself – my entire body was trembling with rage.

I had faced many tribulations since childhood – chief

among them, a shortage of money. Yet I was never much bothered to immediately address that shortage. I always thought that things would take care of themselves in due time. I wanted success in life, but I was not in any hurry. I didn't want success at any cost. Therefore, I had paid the price for not compromising my values. But Zara was different.

Zara had grown up in my own neighbourhood, in a family that was wealthier than ours. She was the daughter of Firoz *chacha* (uncle) and Nadima *chachi* (aunt). As an only child, she had been indulged all her childhood. Her every desire had been fulfilled. She had a bachelor's degree in political science. She was ambitious. She believed our daughter should go to an expensive school. She wanted a house for us. And a car. She believed in upward mobility. But I wasn't much interested in these things. Therefore, our perspectives about the world were different; and so were our approaches on how to lead our lives.

It was quite difficult for Zara to maintain the household. Everything from rent to our daughter's school fees, as well as daily expenses, had increased. It wasn't easy to manage everything. I did understand that. But I was not in any position to do much about it. I had my own problems. I had remained a clerk my whole life. My salary was limited; there were no other sources of income.

Zara and I worked night and day to meet our daily needs. We ran from home to office and then from office to home. There wasn't much in our lives beyond that daily grind. Therefore, we were always stressed – strife and squabble, our fate. In this tension, we could never bring ourselves to discuss our domestic issues with cool heads. Perhaps we were both burdened by our respective egos. I'd become weary of discord with Zara. I wanted a solution to this problem – for good.

I thought long and hard about what to do. One Friday, I bought a silk sari for Zara and a frock for our daughter on my way back from work. I wasn't very adept at making my family members happy by buying them gifts; a colleague at work had suggested I do so. He said that wives were pleased by such gestures. I bought the presents because I thought the advice reasonable, not because of some deep-seated conviction. But, the main reason was that I wanted to send Zara a message – that I understood the issues she had raised and agreed with her.

As soon as I arrived home carrying the gifts, she asked sternly, 'What's in your hands?'

At that moment, it felt as if Zara didn't even want to see my face. I was stunned at seeing her anger. However, I replied gently, 'These are some gifts for you and Ayesha.'

'There is no need for stupid gifts! Why did you buy all this? Where did you find the money to buy these things?' she pressed.

I kept my composure, but lied. 'I had lent some money to a friend a while ago. He repaid me today. I used the money to buy you these presents. Open them – they are nice. They will look good on both of you.' She would have hammered me to death had I told her that I borrowed money from my colleague to buy those gifts.

'Why did you spend money so frivolously? Do we have surplus money?' She was annoyed. 'You can't do one useful thing.'

There was nothing but rejection in Zara's words and actions towards me. I hadn't experienced such behaviour from her before. Her behaviour had changed drastically in the last few months. 'Let's face the main problem here,' she admonished me. 'How are we going to raise the money for Ayesha's wedding? Have you ever thought about that? We have neither ancestral wealth nor any savings.'

I was enraged by her attitude. However, I nodded my head and calmly listened to her. 'You are right,' I said after a while. 'Tell me – what should I do?'

'What can I say? Do I always have to give you advice?' she yelled. 'Can you not think of things yourself?'

'I don't know, Zara. I have done everything I can under the circumstances. I can't think of or do more than that. I am not a man of great abilities. I do what I am told. So please tell me. Have I ever said that I won't do what you ask me to do?' I asked helplessly.

'You don't say you won't. But you also don't listen to what I have to say.'

'Don't say that. I have always heeded you. Now tell me, what should I do?' I tried to charm her.

She was silent for a while before proposing, 'Resign from your job and go to Canada.'

'How did Canada come up all of a sudden?' I was surprised. 'You think it's as simple as moving homes from Lahore to Islamabad?'

'I have long been giving this a thought. I've looked into it and got some information from my friends. They say there are many opportunities there for civil engineers like you. Our problems would be solved if you took even a simple job there. It would be enough. You don't have to worry about us. I will take good care of Ayesha here.'

'Did you say you will raise Ayesha? Without me? I have never been abroad; what am I going to do there at this age? Are you talking sense? How can you suggest such a thing? And why wouldn't you two come along?' I was shocked by her suggestion.

'How can we go? Our daughter will lose her way! Your brain isn't worth two cents. What if she eloped with someone from there? No! I am not willing to raise Ayesha in western culture. She needs to put down her roots here. Don't you want your daughter to marry a Muslim man?' she argued.

'What nonsense are you spewing? I haven't travelled abroad, but I know a few things about Canada. What do you think – that the Muslims who live in Canada don't marry Muslims?' I further asked, 'What do you want our daughter to become? Doesn't she need to understand the outside world?'

'Yes, she does, but only while being connected to her own community. In Canada, we both will have to work. Who is going to look after her then?'

'Why? Has it not been possible here? After all, we both go to work here too,' I countered.

'The whole community raises the children here. Kids

grow up in the laps of relatives. Here the wider society is like our communal family. Western society is not like that. It only consists of individuals,' she answered.

I'd never known that Zara was so well informed about western society. How could I have? We had never spoken on the subject.

'Who will take care of your younger brother Akib?' she continued. 'Regular medication allows you to take care of yourself well. But Akib? He needs a separate caretaker. How can I leave him here?'

Zara's remark made me glad. I thought to myself, 'Bless her! How many would say no to a trip abroad in order to take care of their brother-in-law?'

I didn't allow my satisfaction to surface in front of her. 'I don't agree with you. Don't you want our daughter to go to a good school and university? Canada's universities are world class. Our daughter will get to know the inventions and modern ways of the west – she will learn. Western sensibility leads the world today. And don't worry about Akib. There are good medical facilities in Pakistan to take excellent care of him,' I tried to get her to agree with me.

'All right, I accept your point. But what will I do there? I won't be able to get a job in my profession. I will have to take up any paying job. But I am not willing to become an educated slave. And we can never fully become Canadians. They won't accept us as we are. All they need is labour for their economic system. We sell our labour and earn some wealth. It is purely a transaction of labour and money. The contract between us is clear,' she pressed her point.

'Citizens of Canada receive services from the state. Health care is free. They have a good pension system,' she went one, 'but they also have widespread discrimination – as a foundational institution. Canadian history is full of miseries undergone by the Black, Chinese and south Asian peoples. Immigrants have long been oppressed there. They compared the standard of living in their own nations and then made compromises. But that is a separate issue. In the past, the west wasn't just hungry for material progress; it was also spiritual. Over time, it surrendered to the arrogance of material progress. It lost its spiritual identity. Over time, it became multicultural. The east, however, was satisfied with pluralism. The west chose reason, the east, nature. The west chose life, the east chose life and world, both. Nature gives birth to diverse things. Therefore, diversity is the value of our lives – a natural way of life.'

I didn't agree with Zara. But I was astonished at her ability to debate. A person cannot debate without knowledge. She clearly had knowledge of not only our own society but also of western society.

I put forth my arguments again, 'I disagree with your understanding of Canadian society. I have read about it. It is not like other western societies. Please don't falsely accuse Canadian society of discrimination. Canadians are extremely friendly and gracious. They help everyone, be it migrants or refugees. More than two hundred ethnicities live there in harmony. South Asians are among the biggest minorities there.'

'What does Pakistan have?' I added. 'Here life has no

value. The food is poisonous. The very air we breathe is noxious. Societal and communal relationships are toxic. Everyone gets a poisoned life in their share. Everyone is divided into clans and tribes. Everyone hates everyone. "I am more important than him! That one is lesser than that one!" – what shall we call this psychological slavery? A few chosen families govern the country. Countless are made destitute. How can I leave you and Ayesha alone in this environment? Please reconsider your decision,' I poured out my feelings in that request.

'Who doesn't discriminate?' I added. 'Can you show me a nation that does not discriminate? Who doesn't want to consolidate power in their own hands? Who isn't hiding their true self behind a mask, Zara? Aren't you hiding? Aren't I? Does any society permit its people to walk around naked? Without some kind of a mask or cover? We are all draped in our own burqas.'

'When have we not donned a mask of some kind, whether of principles, or religion, or culture, or of tradition? Doesn't our society actually have a larger and more frightening chasm? Have we ever been self-reflective about our own society? It is easy to criticize others, but self-evaluation is difficult. We have become ignorant. There's nothing Pakistan can give us, Zara. So, let's all go away from here.' I tried to emphasize my points.

I am not quite sure how I managed to say all those things. My breath felt heavy; my body was trembling. It was as if I wasn't debating but fighting. But before I was able to gather myself, Zara responded:

'Pakistan has given me my being – the meaning to my existence. Yes, our society is not without its problems, but I feel that my life finds meaning here. I feel proud. This pride is a gift from my tradition. I won't say that tradition alone is preeminent, but I also don't consider it expendable. I don't consider my traditions to be the past. They are alive with me in my present. Yet we call this vibrant stream primitive. All in the name of progress; in the name of development. As if the past held no developments. As if the traditions of the truths established by Mohammed and the Sufi weren't progressive at all!'

Zara was speaking very serenely. Like a philosopher. I had never seen her in this guise. Her eyes had a strange sparkle. I couldn't find the courage to look into that radiance. Trying to avoid her eyes, I asked, 'If that is indeed the case, then why are you pushing me alone towards Canada? Don't I also have the right to live in my own village, my own society?'

Zara had become calm by then. 'I am asking for your help,' she explained. 'Our financial situation is bad. We have to overcome this difficulty; rise above the present circumstance. We can start our own savings from the money you send us. Plus, you aren't going to be gone forever. This is just a temporary arrangement. This makes no one happy – it will be difficult for us without you. But you can return as soon as our situation starts to improve.'

Zara fell silent after that. I too remained quiet. There was nothing more to say. We had exchanged all our knowledge, experience, and bitterness with each other. I couldn't counter Zara. I surrendered before her reasoning ability. It wasn't in my nature to surrender – especially to my wife – but I did it anyway.

There was a reason for it. I wanted to be alone. Away from Zara and Ayesha. Away from discord and disharmony. Liberated from day-to-day responsibilities; free from Zara's daily nagging. I was exhausted by everything. I was looking for something – a new place where I could live carefree. I saw an opportunity in Zara's proposition – an opportunity for self-exploration – for self-exile.

Then I thought, 'What will people think if they find out about me?'

Maybe they'll say, 'What kind of a lunatic is he? Sometimes he yearns to live with his whole family while at other times looks for solitude away from them! He sometimes chooses society and crowds, then at other times, he chooses exile.'

I am sure if anyone was aware of this contradiction within me, they would be astonished.

But then I asked myself again, 'What is so surprising about this? Don't we all live with some kind of duality? With a bit of lunacy?'

'Contradiction is an integral part of all of us. Perhaps it is man's pure and essential character. Man doesn't embrace contradiction by choice. It emerges at birth and disappears at death. It's just that only some people recognize this. Most others don't. Some accept it; others don't'

This very recognition had become the main complication of my life. It compelled me to seek out the purpose of living. I don't remember when this question of existence took root within me, but it had defined and distilled my personality to a great extent. However, caught in life's day-to-day concerns, I had long repressed this question somewhere inside me.

No one in the modern world has any time to consider these questions. Because the present society declares those in search of life's meaning 'directionless' – aimless. They are called vagabonds – vagrants. In this age when all communities, societies, and nations blindly run after a singular aim – power consolidation, how could I live without any 'direction'?

People say – 'This is the age of the individual. A person has the right to live exactly how he wants.' But this is not the whole truth. Because man doesn't truly have the permission to seek out alternatives. He just has the allowance to choose between pre-provided options. Like a caged parrot. It's able to fly but only within the confines of the cage. In the end the parrot slowly but surely is diminished.

Isn't civilization today similarly cramped and bogged down? Humanity is looking for freedom – from those present-day ideas that in the name of liberty have robbed humanity of its dreams. Yet civilization today is so helpless and paralyzed that it cannot counteract the norms it has created itself. For want of knowledge and conscience. This conscience will now be borne by a new age. And in the throes of that birth, the age will ask for another sacrifice. Of the common man. Of his dreams. The earth will be bathed in blood. After a century, this process will be repeated.

It is an uninterrupted process – man's life, the life of a civilization, revolutions, change, corpses, blood, sacrifice – continuous, uninterrupted. The earth is an abattoir; man is a holy offering prepared for sacrifice. Everywhere death performs its terrifying dance.

I couldn't fall asleep that night. Zara and Ayesha had fallen asleep after dinner, but I had many thoughts running through my mind. I thought about my past – thought about my parents, and my ancestors. I thought about their struggles; about their journey. These memories, attached to man's life, are strange – friends in solitude; balm in pain; strength in weakness. Events from my past danced before my eyes one after another.

My ancestors led a wandering life – moving from one country to another. They didn't stay for long in any one place. They arrived in Afghanistan from eastern Iran. My grandfather moved from Afghanistan to Jalandhar in India. He remained in Jalandhar until the partition in 1947; after which he moved to Lahore. I was born in Lahore and grew up here.

My relationship with Lahore was very intimate – unconstrained by time. I discovered myself many times over in the verdant environs of the city. Countless stories from my childhood are etched in its alleyways. I feel I am somehow a part of every fragment of this city's history. Its future will not be able to erase my footprint. I shall forever remain alive in its womb.

This place was always heaven to me. I remember holding my father's hand as a child on our many trips to the 'Hazrat Data Ganj Bakhsh Ali Hujwiri' shrine. Memories of trips with friends to the 'Pak tea house' still excite me. I used to roam around Anarkali, Bano Bazaar, Rang Mahal and Liberty Market with those same friends. Our whole family used to go to 'Mohammad Nihari' to eat *nihari* (stew made from meat). My past feels no more distant than yesterday to me.

Each generation loves its birthplace and the people in it, and maintains an attachment to it. It interprets its connection to the place in its own way. I too had done likewise. My childhood was spent playing cricket in its alleyways. Those alleys and my childhood friends are still rooted in my heart – their memory perfumed like sandalwood.

Relatives and older friends from college, however, loathed me. They abandoned me. And betrayed me. Despite that, I craved their love and tried hard to obtain it – constantly – like a thirsty deer. Relationships are like that. Some are loving, some loathsome. Some require surrender, some sacrifice. Some are candid, others deceitful.

I have acquired numerous relationships in my life. I have lost many as well. I still remember some of them; some, however, have disappeared from memory. Memories of my first love Awida still surface from time to time – childhood love isn't so easily forgotten. It wasn't possible in a society like ours to have a relationship while still in school. It was dangerous. Yet, I always stepped out of the house to catch a glimpse of her. I used to follow her in secret.

Unlike other girls, Awida didn't wear a burqa. I was bewitched by her smile as if under a dark spell. Fair and slender, Awida was extremely attractive. I found her dynamic, like monsoon streams. Those days, I used to talk to her endlessly in my dreams – hold her hands and express my love for her. However, in reality, I never mustered up the courage to speak to her. I was afraid that she would tell on me to my father. I don't think she ever found out that I loved her. Later, when time had passed, I didn't think it opportune any more to tell her about it.

Perhaps there's truth to the saying – 'Time heals all wounds.' A few years after school, Awida's image, once deeply etched in my heart, started to fade away. Like a morning shrouded in fog, I became absorbed in other things. As I grew older, the expectations from family and society to become sensible and prudent bore down on me. Questions like what to do and what to become in life took priority. I began to rid myself of the feelings I had so lovingly nourished as a child. In this process, I also freed myself from Awida.

From that point in my life, I relinquished all sentimentality. I renounced love; abandoned my essence – in order to commence my journey towards modernity, to become successful. The desire for success compelled me to be self-centred and arrogant. But today, as a result, I have become a ruin, fragmented into parts – a remnant that possesses a life, but has become lifeless because it lacks a bridge to connect its past and present.

After successfully seeing off Awida from my life, I entered university in 1982. Thus started a new chapter in my life, filled with fantasies. I dreamt of marrying the most popular beauty on campus. I also started developing notions about disrupting power through student politics. I wanted to rise up against the injustice widespread in Pakistani society.

It was a matter of the heart after all – a young heart at that. Why would it listen to anyone but itself? Without a thought to the consequences, I started organizing protests on campus, giving speeches against the government. I wanted to be famous. I yearned to be praised. By Razia. I used to think that she was the most beautiful woman on campus – yes, Razia was! What is it that they say? – 'Things change, but things remain the same.' I discarded all the logic I had leaned on in order to forget Awida, in order to let Razia into my heart. As it is, most people decide what to embrace and abandon in life based on their own circumstances, and love's desire cannot be defeated by the crutches of reason. Love is sharper than a sword. Its blade destroys everything – mind, morality, reason, reflection. My love for Razia began with such a destruction of myself.

1982 was a time of upheaval in Pakistani politics. In 1981, eleven political parties formed an alliance against the authoritarian government of Muhammad Zia-ul-Haq. It was called the 'Movement for the Restoration of Democracy'. This alliance had started a populist movement in support of democracy. Various fraternal youth organizations connected to various parties were preparing for the student elections coming up in 1983. The left-leaning progressive student alliance was predicted to win. Suppression by the government was rife. Pakistan was at the centre of political upheaval. And I, a revolutionary member, was ready to dive into that tumult.

I was in double turmoil at that time. Razia had taken over my heart and mind. She'd become an important part of my life before I even realized it. I'd heard that youth required no reason to love; turned out it was true. Especially when it came to someone as beautiful as Razia. She dressed in a distinct way, and had a special personality – a personality that revealed her social class. In Lahore of the 80s, the tussle between Islamization and modernization was at its zenith. In such a society and under these circumstances, she was a progressive woman who didn't wear the burqa. She seemed radiant as if bathed in moonlight. Like the actress Shabnam from the popular 1977 film *Aaina*.

We were in the same batch. Yet, introvert that I was, I hadn't mustered up the courage to speak to her. I could neither introduce myself to her, nor had anyone else done me the favour of introducing us to each other. I used to secretly admire her from afar. Razia's friends had gotten wind of this fact. They started teasing Razia about me. Sometimes Razia would look in my direction and smile. I would get nervous and pretend I hadn't seen it. But I was getting more and more desperate about her. I used to wander her neighbourhood – not without anxiety – just to catch a glimpse of her. But there was a certain sweetness to that fear. I was prepared to face any danger to be able to speak to her.

One day I decided to skip classes at college. I wanted to use that as an excuse to talk to her – by asking her for lecture notes. As planned, I didn't attend classes that day. I still remember running to the campus in anticipation the next day. But she wasn't there. I was very restless that day – angry at the clock that seemed to move ever so slowly.

The following day, she appeared before me like bright sunlight. The previous day's anger turned into joy. Like the morning sunlight that striates a rocky mountain into untold dimensions, her eyes carved me into pieces. I melted. I lost all sense of who I was. When a man loses his identity, there's nothing more he has to lose – he is ready for anything. I too was ready.

Standing in front of her, I said, 'Razia, I was unable to come to campus the other day. Will you please share your notes from 'Intro to Engineering'?

'Of course!' she said, and gave me her notes.

That moment when I first spoke with her is fixed in my heart to this day.

After that I took every opportunity to talk to her. She responded openly on her part. Sometimes I used to ask her about her plans after her studies. And sometimes I asked her if she had a boyfriend. I always found excuses to talk to her. She used to get embarrassed when I asked her if she had a boyfriend.

'Why is she so coy?' I wondered.

'Perhaps she is also interested in me,' I would think and get excited.

Things started to gradually change for me. I myself

was going through changes. It had been some time since I'd started talking to Razia. That gave me more courage. I decided to express my love for her and waited for the right time.

Spring had arrived. One day, I saw her alone in the garden on campus. She seemed to be deep in thought. Deciding that this was the right time, I gathered up all my courage, appeared before her, and asked, 'Razia, I want to talk to you about something. Are you free?'

'Is it important?' she asked.

'Nothing is as important to me as this.'

'Then I am free. What is it?'

I got a bit spooked. I worried about what she might think after listening to what I had to say. My mouth went dry. I was stuck.

'What's the matter?' she asked again.

Everything before me started to dim. I got lost in the darkness for a bit. But her voice pulled me out and I quickly blurted out, 'I love you Razia. I want to marry you.'

She didn't say anything. She kept staring into my eyes. She knew that I liked her. But maybe she didn't anticipate that I would propose to her. Those days, it wasn't simple to propose to a woman. Perhaps she couldn't believe me.

'But how? Why?' she asked in a subdued voice. Then, more sternly, she said, 'Ali, you are my friend. I haven't thought of anything more than that.'

'Can friends not love each other, Razia? It's okay if you haven't given it much thought, but please think about it now. Do you know how much I love you? I have loved you from the moment I saw you,' my voice trembled.

'Ali, it's nice to hear that someone loves you. But I don't love you. Please try to understand my point of view. I have much to achieve in life. I need to accomplish my goals. I want to get somewhere; be somebody. This is the time to focus on studies. I want to graduate with good grades.' Her voice was full of determination.

'But I promise not to hold you back from your ambitions,' I pleaded.

'This is not possible, Ali,' she said and with that she left.

My heart was cleaved. I couldn't sleep that night. Razia's figure continued dancing in front of me. I embraced her image and kept shedding tears. Her eyes kept staring at me that night. I implored those hypnotic eyes – 'Hey light of my eyes, please don't leave me.' But she disappeared. And for a long time, a weight on my chest made me feel as if I couldn't breathe. The pain of separation has its own saga – I only understood that day.

Some people meet each other for only a short time. Yet sometimes, that short encounter stays long in memory. Through Razia, I had experienced unrequited love; I had experienced pain. I believe that pain is a cardinal truth of life. And to this day, I am grateful to the goddess who brought me face to face with that truth. Many women came into my life after Razia. Some gave me pain while others left me with sweet memories. Razia remained with me as a fractured portion of my entire existence. A memory that is still alive. I still feel the magnetic pull of her dazzling eyes.

Many years later, I came to know that Razia's parents had pressured her into marrying against her wishes. 'How did such a progressive woman not manage to resist her parents?' I wondered. 'That too for a match with a person who had a criminal background!' Perhaps she'd had her own difficulties and complications. Turns out the parents hadn't known about the groom's criminal background until much later. Hearing all that made me quite worried about her.

What a misfortune! Perhaps if she'd had a way of knowing her future, she wouldn't have rejected my proposal. But who can see the future? Numerous predictions about the future, from even the greatest scholars, have proved useless. Razia was but a simple student. How could she have seen into her future, besides dreaming a beautiful dream? Her reality had turned her dream into ashes. I scattered the ashes of Razia's dream in a safe corner of my heart, as if they were my own dreams, and moved on in life.

I graduated with a bachelor's degree in engineering in 1986. Then I worked as a clerk in government service for fourteen years. I'd gone to Canada after resigning from this very job. Till then, I had spent every moment of my life in Lahore, therefore, whatever I had become in life, it was because of Lahore. All my life, I've yearned for the time I spent there. Like a child insisting that he should have the moon, I always longed for those times.

People remain intimately connected with their youth and the events that took place then. We all have our own perceptions of time; we evolve in a particular manner, and maintain ourselves in a particular state. That particular state and the particular time define us. They construct and deconstruct us. Only time is certain. The rest is uncertain. We are but emissaries who dance for a predetermined time – ephemeral like the melody of a flute. Perhaps we call that melody life.

Filled with the enthusiasm and vigour of youth, I used to think that I had deeply absorbed the era and events in Lahore – internalized them. That same energy had deepened my love for Lahore. In years gone by, these feelings and ideas were ascendant in my heart; predominant in my mind. I was leaving behind this capital I had earned over a lifetime when I left for Canada. I didn't know if I was making the right decision or not. But I felt hollow deep within myself.

I wonder how my father would have reacted, had he been still alive, to the news that I was going to Canada. I still remember the conversations I used to have with him. Once, he told me, 'Ali, the history of human civilization is shaped by the history of human migration. People have long been migrating in search of a better life – from one place to another. They became familiar with different circumstances. They became whatever their time, era, environment and circumstance made them. They came up with new inventions based on place and need. They gave birth to knowledge. Then they bestowed that hard earned knowledge and experience to newer generations. The knowledge and culture I have, I received from my ancestors. And I have handed over what I know to you.

And in turn, you will hand over to your progeny. The world endures as a legacy of the past. This process is extremely important for the development of our civilization. There is no such thing that is completely modern. All inventions are traditional. A complete divorce from history has been possible only in a few important eras. Therefore, modernity is a belief wrapped up in tradition – one that attempts to make itself legitimate by refining itself according to new circumstances. Therefore, modernity and tradition live side by side. Strengthening each other. Don't think that our modernity is novel. Look closely at its source. Tradition migrates from one particular place to another and takes on the form of modernity. Look carefully – everyone and everything changes location. Perhaps not geographically, but intellectually, culturally. We have all migrated in some way and will continue to do so.'

After all these years, I still remember my father's furrowed face when he explained the importance of migration. I think, at that moment, he was feeling that emptiness that migration brings along with it. Perhaps he was remembering all those places and people who had been a part of his life before he settled in Lahore. Perhaps he was traumatized by his loneliness. I had made the decision to go to Canada after my father was long gone. Had he been still alive, I think he would have expressed neither happiness nor sadness at that decision.

It is difficult to understand one's parents. They are somewhat mysteriously entangled in their children's lives. They can neither hide everything, nor completely express themselves. They neither want to hold on to us forever, nor can they let go of us completely.

I was the eldest son of the family. I had a very close relationship with my father. He was a friend to me for as long as he lived. He never ceased to pat me on the back even when I couldn't get good grades in school. I used to hug him and place my head on his shoulder, and amidst tears, promise that I would do better next time. I could never get good grades. But I also didn't stop crying or making promises. But my father always shielded me from the guilt of failure. When he left this world, I was deeply stricken. As a matter of fact, from that day to now, I haven't been able to stand on my own feet. I have just gone along with the flow of time's current. Hobbling along.

In the end, I decided to hobble once more. I quickly made the decision to go to Canada.

I left for Canada in 2000. Zara was content to stay in Pakistan. Zara and Ayesha came to the airport to see me off. Before leaving, I robotically repeated to Zara, 'I would have been happy if you and Ayesha were coming along with me.'

She replied without a moment's hesitation, 'Let's not say any more about this. Please be cheerful as you go.'

'Alright. Take care of yourself and our daughter. Goodbye.'

'Goodbye, Ali. Don't forget to call when you arrive in Canada.'

'Of course.'

And with that I departed for Canada.

Experience

I arrived in Toronto in the summer. I had to make a fresh start; had to learn new ways. I was excited but also anxious. I was apprehensive about the turns my life would take in this new place. My childhood friend, Aahil, was picking me up at the airport. Aahil and I had gone to the same school in Lahore. We were very close – he was the only one who knew about my childhood crushes. We had lost touch after he moved to Canada, and I was curious to see how Aahil had changed after so many years.

I spotted Aahil after a short while. He had gained some weight, but his face hadn't changed much. It had a few wrinkles. They seemed to me the result of life's disappointments – there was a deep weariness about him. We hugged each other tightly and let ourselves be washed over by emotion. Then we composed ourselves and asked after each other's health and families. Aahil then drove us towards the flat where he lived.

I looked out the car window. Toronto in summer looked like art on a painter's canvas – lending itself to multiple interpretations – beautiful; calm; constant. There were gardens everywhere, and in them, flowers of every kind. The entire city was covered in greenery. I quietly stared out the window. Before my mind could be satiated by the parade of artistic vistas appearing before my eyes, Aahil informed me that we had reached home.

We had arrived at 240 Wellesley Street East. I ended up staying at the same address my entire time in Canada. It was a high rise in the downtown area. Aahil was on the seventh floor. His wife, Hasita, welcomed me at the door. Hasita was about the same age as Zara. But a bit more cheerful; a bit more easy-going; also a bit more attractive. Theirs was a family of three – Aahil, Hasita and their son, Baber. They had lived in Toronto for ten years. Baber was just a school kid when they'd arrived; now he was in the first year of his bachelor's at Toronto University.

Aahil and Hasita both worked. Their life had been moving along on the same track for years – go to work in the morning; return in the evening; cook, eat, prepare for the following day; and repeat. They hadn't fully assimilated but were well on their way.

'You made exactly the right decision by arriving in the summer,' Hasita struck up a conversation.

I was glad that Hasita had broken the ice. Until I

arranged a flat for myself, I had no choice but to stay with Aahil's family. Guests quickly become a burden abroad. I knew I was one. But I still wanted to impose as little as possible on them. Therefore, it was necessary to maintain a good relationship with them – especially with Hasita. I also wasn't sure how much Aahil had changed after so many years. But as it is, people aren't good or bad in themselves – their circumstances are what can be good or bad.

Seeing me lost in thought, Hasita tried to draw me into a conversation. 'Are Zara and Ayesha well? Your daughter must be quite grown up by now. Why didn't they come with you?'

'They are doing well. Yes, our daughter is growing up really fast,' I responded. 'I'm sure you are aware of Akib's illness. We couldn't leave him alone. So they stayed back in Pakistan,' I couldn't be open with Hasita about Zara's position on Canadian society.

'That's right!' Hasita rejoined, 'I totally forgot about Akib. I haven't met him, but I do know about him. Aahil has told me. He does need someone responsible to take care of him. You made the correct decision. I especially approve of your decision to come to Canada in the summer. There are more job opportunities available at this time. You shouldn't let them go. Everyone leaves their past behind on arriving here. There's no use in holding on to what one did back in the home country. One should take the first job one gets. Here your work is your creed – your office, your mosque.'

I wondered why she was putting so much emphasis on

work. Perhaps she was trying to suggest that, abroad, one shouldn't be a guest at others' for too long.

I wasn't too worried by her implied message, however. I myself had no intention of being a burden on them. There's nothing more important to me than my independence. I have never wanted to be a burden on anyone. Not even on my own self. But wanting something doesn't make it so; a man has to carry his own burden for a lifetime.

Seeing me somewhat distracted, Aahil spoke up, 'Hasita, don't overwhelm him. He's just arrived today. He will learn the ways here soon enough.'

'Don't be so derisive, Aahil,' Hasita was quick to respond. 'Don't embarrass me in front of Ali. I have no objection to him staying here for as long as he wants. He can feel at home here. I was just trying to help him.'

'I agree with you completely, Hasita,' I intervened.

After dinner we retired to our beds. Because of the jetlag, I couldn't fall asleep for a long time. But as darkness enveloped the night, I fell asleep without realizing it. Even in that sleep, the inner voice that long haunted me echoed again. 'Wake up, Ali. You have been asleep for a lifetime. Now wake up.'

The next day when I woke up, Aahil and Hasita had already left for work. I didn't feel like going out that day. I spent time at home – had breakfast; made lunch; did the dishes. In a foreign land, I found it easy to do household chores. I would likely have moaned and groaned if I'd had to do the same work in Pakistan. I don't know why it was easier in Canada. Perhaps because everything was easily accessible in the small kitchen.

Aahil and Hasita came home in the evening. Baber hadn't returned yet. Aahil was complaining about the city – perhaps because he was tired. Hasita, on the other hand, smiled at me. Eying the kitchen, she said, 'Why did you bother cleaning the kitchen? I would have done it,' with practiced formality. Her countenance, however, was appreciative.

'It's not a bother to do chores around the house,' I said. 'It's the same regardless of whether you do it or I do it.'

'Did you help Zara around the house like this in Lahore as well?' Hasita asked promptly with a laugh.

Unable to answer, I tried to avoid Hasita's eyes. But her eyes kept following me – like they were trying to say something else. I felt uncomfortable. Perhaps sensing my discomfort, Aahil suggested that we go out to see the sights.

Later that evening, we went out for a bit of sightseeing.

Strolling around in Wellesley Park, I found everything extremely beautiful. Serene. As if man and nature had come together to form a coherent whole. As if together they were contemplating on the sources of their very lives. As if the warmth of summer had imbued them with joy. Birds were singing their melodies. The blooming tulips in the park seemed capable of completely rejuvenating humanity. I found everyone content; captivated. Enveloped within themselves.

'Feels like ages since the sun has come out,' Aahil said, breaking the quiet. 'Nine months of unpredictable weather and cold makes people deeply weary. Makes one feel totally enervated. I find this place cold at all times except for July and August. This is the best time in Toronto. Baber wishes that this weather would never go away.'

'You're right! What greenery – and beauty – everywhere! I feel like my romance with this city has already begun,' I declared.

Surprised at myself, I added, 'Aahil, looks like there are a lot of Pakistanis living here.'

'Yes. There are a few Pakistanis. And some Nepalis too. But there are many people from other countries living here as well. This neighbourhood is in the centre of Toronto. Rent is a bit high here in comparison to other places, but it's very convenient to live in. There are many job opportunities; transportation is easy; and the market is close by. Therefore, new arrivals in town prefer to live here,' Aahil explained.

I didn't ask anything else. After wandering around a bit, we headed home.

I hadn't started working yet, so I had quite a bit of free time. I started to study the lives of the residents there. It was easy to make their acquaintance – they initiated conversations whenever they saw a new person. They could easily identify new arrivals from Pakistan. They always came up and asked, 'Are you from Pakistan? What province of Pakistan are you from?' During the summer, it was their daily routine to gather in groups at the Rose Avenue Public School and Wellesley Park.

I used to participate in their discussions. Pakistan's

politics was a perennial subject. They'd be melancholic at the memory of their home, society and their past. They'd hold political leaders responsible for their misery and berate those leaders the most. But, they would also gossip about someone or the other – criticize them and make fun.

I used to wonder, 'Why so much criticism – of politics, society, others, everything? Criticism in every direction!'

Democratic progressives say, 'Criticism is the lifeblood of the civilized world.' Perhaps. But the constant criticisms from prosperous people seemed like petty grievances. Like compulsive complaining to make up for feelings of dissatisfaction. But not everyone had time to chatter in that manner. Those who had good jobs never took part in these discussions; they didn't find it necessary to be a part of such a group. Those who were new arrivals didn't have any free time from chasing a job or running after school. Only those who were neither fully settled nor totally unsettled had free time for these discussions.

Aahil and I went around town at every opportunity. I loved seeing new places, and Aahil loved showing me around. On one of those days, Aahil recounted his experiences during his early days in Canada. I still remember him saying, 'It was very difficult to get used to the freezing cold here. It wasn't like we didn't experience cold in Pakistan but never like this. The cold here is daunting. We had neither relatives nor any friends at that time. We didn't know what to do. Didn't have any idea where to start. We didn't have jobs. The money we had brought from Pakistan was getting spent – how long would that money have lasted?

We were so desperate we entertained the idea of returning to Pakistan. But how could we return without losing face. Our relatives had seen us off with many congratulations on becoming permanent residents of Canada. How could we return without any achievements?'

'I can understand,' I said. 'It obviously takes some time to get used to a new place. That too in a place like Canada. It's doubly difficult if you don't have a job here.'

'Pakistani society is in a downward spiral right now,' I said with a sigh. 'Our thinking is becoming troubling. We consider it a success to move abroad. We consider it a special advancement to move to a western country. The social attitude in most countries trying to emulate the west is exactly this. Our society is oppressed by our own selves. We are rewarding the corrupt. The honest are being made fools of. Criminals have taken over politics. Ones with money have no problems moving ahead. The middle class is losing its ability to rid the country of primitive ideas; it has merely turned into an automaton for making money.'

'Yesterday's class struggle has morphed into a personal struggle today,' I added. 'It has turned into communal and caste struggles. Man has been thrown into these struggles all at once – with the stated desire to make human life and values more advanced. But in reality, man has become more fragmented – more scattered. It's as if his life force has been extinguished. There are neither artists to fill people's souls nor are there any sages like Rumi. Man is therefore lost. And no one is willing to search for the lost man in this day and age. On the other hand, people are trapped in the quagmire of unjust systems – ironically, caught in the whirlpool of the very systems that were created to liberate them. Systems trap us. Therefore, the claim that new systems created in new eras make people freer is a myth. People have been taking the myths to be truths. They have been living according to these myths. And dying by the same.'

'You speak the truth, Ali,' Aahil said after listening to me, 'but it is not easy here either. You have to work day and night in order to survive. Everything you earn is spent paying rent, phone, electricity, and other bills. You can save a small amount if you are lucky. But you have to devote night and day in order to provide good opportunities for your children. After all, what is all this sacrifice for? And it is inevitable that you are alone in your old age. The children to whom you devote each day and night go their own way. I see a lot of Canadians spend their old age alone. "Loneliness" is a word that sends shivers down my spine. I think I should return to Pakistan soon instead of being alone here. Let's see what happens. Here, all relationships feel mechanized. At least in Pakistan I won't die alone.'

The word Aahil emphasized, 'alone,' resonated in my ears for a long time. I also started becoming afraid of that word.

Seeing me lost in thought, Aahil asked, 'What are you thinking, Ali?'

Discomfited, I responded, 'I don't agree with you, Aahil. In the end, everyone dies alone – whether in Pakistan or Canada. In either place people will come to your funeral. Some will be there because they love you, others because of social pressure. People maintain relationships for varying reasons. In today's age where relationships have become transactions, the methods of carrying on relationships are the same almost everywhere. Canada and Pakistan aren't much different from each other. People are the same everywhere – governed by nature's rules and their own passions.

'It's not right to blame anyone else for our circumstances in Canada,' I added, 'because life means compromise. You take something with one hand and give something with the other. This is how things work. There are certain advantages to living in Toronto, and there are others of living in Pakistan. No one is forcing you to live here. It's your own decision. Look at me – I had a perfectly fine job in Pakistan. Yet I chose to come here. I should be willing to endure the difficulties resulting from my decision, shouldn't I?'

'You're right, Ali. Whether you migrate or not is an individual decision. But you can't call it a totally free decision. I was forced to migrate. My country's politics does not look after a middle class person like me. But our country's politics itself isn't free. It is heavily influenced by international systems and processes.'

'We grew up in turbulent times. But we believed that things would get better. But where is the change? Nothing has changed so far. Nor will it ever change. Circumstances are getting worse. What kind of times are we living in? What kind of age are we going to be a part of? We couldn't be happy in Pakistan, nor are we in Canada. We are trapped in the vortex of our own desire... shame! It would've helped if the Canadian government had done something at least to ease our troubles. It hasn't done even that. A lot of non-profit organizations work on immigrant issues. Yet they don't understand the value of work experience in Pakistan. They don't understand the nature of work there. So how can they help us then? Why is it so difficult for capable people to find work here? They claim Canada's economy is very strong. The ironic thing is that the very people who were recruited under the category of "skilled immigrants" make up the ranks of the unemployed.'

'Aahil, I think the root of the problem is in the attitudes of Canadians and non-Canadians; in their understanding of work; in their point of view towards life. We live simultaneously in the past, present, and future. They live in the present and future. While we are guided by religion, tradition, emotion and reason, they are mostly guided by emotion and reason. We are from different cultures. The context in which we grew up in Pakistan or the experiences we gathered there are completely different from the context and experiences here.

'Therefore, the work experience we gained there doesn't hold much value here,' I added. 'However, we can't say that it is completely useless. There are some universal principles of work. They are applicable in Canada as well as in Pakistan. However, familiarity with them alone will not help those organizations to open all doors for us. But, they cannot completely close them either. There has to be some kind of balance.'

'Balance is an inflexible word, Ali. It's not easy to

achieve. Civilizations have fallen because of their inability to find a balance between ambition and greed. Many great wars have been waged. Emperors have lost their pre-eminence because of it.'

'It's certainly difficult, Aahil,' I responded. 'Look carefully at people's lives. Is it easy? Do you find your own life easy? We consider ourselves powerful because of our ambitions, passions and wealth. As if we could move mountains. Or win wars. But is man really that strong? He is nothing but the air he breathes. The moment he loses connection to that air, his life ends. Yet, before that parting, he is strong, and arrogant.'

'Therefore life is powerful, but also weak,' I continued. 'It is expansive, but also narrow. Man's life blossoms in the border between generosity and pettiness. Therefore, man is a superior creation. A creation that requires a lifetime in order to become balanced. So imagine how long it will take a nation to find balance. Yet, we shouldn't stop trying, don't you think?'

Aahil nodded his head in agreement. After that we didn't speak. The sun was beginning to descend to its depths. Dusk appeared in front of our eyes in an extremely beautiful form – and the earth and sky both seemed intoxicated by her embrace. We were speechless. There was joy in that silence; there was pleasure. But as the darkness of the night began to swallow that beautiful summer evening of Toronto, our feet automatically headed towards home.

Days went by, and my desire to get to know Toronto even better increased with time. I started roaming the alleys of Wellesley Street East alone. I was amazed by how well the city was organized. I was enchanted by the alluring monuments of the city; they seemed to be representing a particular era in history – as if they were expressing the human emotions of a past life; as if those past societies were still alive.

Wellesley Street is a neighbourhood within Cabbagetown. Cabbagetown has its own history. Irish families escaping the famine of 1840 had settled there. They used to grow cabbage and other vegetables in their kitchen garden in order to supplement their food requirements in lean times. That is how the entire neighbourhood came to be called Cabbagetown. The neighbourhood remained a slum until the 1970s-80s when it was developed into its present form.

The buildings there bore the Victorian style – two or three stories tall with triangular roofs. The rooms were narrow but the houses looked like mansions from the outside. Indigenous and mixed race people – especially the many famous people who have contributed to Canadian social and political movements – lived in the neighbourhood. With enchanting scenes on the streets and colourful culture, Wellesley Street was a vibrant neighbourhood.

The residents of the neighbourhood seemed free of worries, as if they had come to an agreement with the natural and usual complexities of life. Perhaps because the light of modern knowledge influenced each aspect of life, they didn't carry expectations for more acquisition. They seemed secure and peaceful – like they weren't in a rush for anything. They appreciated life's own pace. And everything they did seemed to reflect their love and respect for their past.

Canadians took pride in their past. They saw themselves somewhere in their own past. They took care of their homes, streets and their streetcars. They planted trees in front of their houses, and looked after their gardens. They conserved any historical looking thing – I never saw any relic being neglected. But they also held a critical view towards history. While they respected the past, they never forgot to question each aspect. Contradiction is perhaps an enduring nature of each society.

The state, for its part, was responsible towards its citizens. It provided its citizens with various welfare programs. It didn't allow its citizens to die for a lack of food or shelter. It was a nation that believed in social democracy. Therefore, a strong relationship had been established between the state and citizens. Citizens respected their state. However, I had my doubts whether it was really a functional state, because I had a different view about functionality. I see functionality in continual chaos – perhaps because I grew up in chaos.

Canadian society was well organized. But, I didn't consider total organization to be good in itself – especially when I saw the Canadian elderly wandering alone in the streets. My heart cried. I wondered, 'How they must feel about staying in government-arranged housing? How they must miss their children? How do they reflect on their own lives? Has the concept of family become so strange? Have grandfathers and grandmothers become valueless?'

Today's economic man has been shedding his social responsibilities. The two most important pillars for constructing a family – love and respect – have been dissolved. We have come to believe that responsibility towards family is characteristic of a primitive society. What is primitive? What is modern? Can there be no harmony between the old and the new?

Some say harmony is a dream. A story created in self-defence by those who cannot make decisions – a mere narrative. A weak person's weapon. Harmony is impossible – life is built on transactions. The feudal economy was diseased. It stood for the benefit of only a limited few. Isn't it precisely for that reason we got rid of it and entered the capitalist system? Didn't we sever our ties with the land on the principles of capitalism?

Was it correct for man to sever his ties with the land? Isn't life anchored to the earth, the soil? Isn't it the very place where we peacefully rest after death? Isn't life the intimate stream that remains, at every moment, in the embrace of soil's love? Yet, why have we abandoned the earth? Is individual freedom unachievable without the sacrifice of the responsibilities of the past?

In reality, life is but an attempt at harmony. Harmony between standing and falling; between breath and death; knowledge and faith. Harmony between revolution and peace; between past and present; tradition and progress; between science and religion; between happiness and sorrow. If one looks closely, there is nothing in this world but harmony.

Yet, man fails to find balance – because he's been taught only 'survival of the fittest.' Meaning, just one truth. According to this truth, only one who remains powerful will survive – only that ideology that remains progressive can survive; the class that remains dominant will survive; the culture that remains advanced will survive. Therefore, in order to survive, it is essential to remain advanced, powerful and progressive. And so a narrative of the powerful, progressive and advanced is developed against the weak, traditional and impoverished.

Those who are divided into the two segments of this narrative remain in constant struggle against each other. One restricts the other – one sees its advancement in the other's ruin. Therefore, today's man has sacrificed tradition. Without doing so, he cannot get close to science. He does not concede the fact that science cannot reveal all of nature's mysteries. Therefore, man is preoccupied day and night trying to make himself the 'fittest' because his entire struggle is for his survival. However, man is cursed to remain alone until he changes his tune from 'survival of the fittest' to 'survival of all' – alone in his own arrogance. He won't understand harmony until then.

Deep in thought, trying to arrive at some sort of a conclusion, I heard someone call out to me – 'Ali!' It was Ranjan calling out to me. Ranjan Khatiwada, who had immigrated from Nepal, also lived on 240 Wellesley Street East. We had met just a few days ago. Learning that he worked at a department store, I had told him that I was also looking for a job.

'How are you, Ranjan? Wandering about? Looks like you are free today.'

'Not really. On my way to buy some vegetables. Can't really say that I get a lot of free time, but I stopped because I saw you. I talked to my store manager about a job for you. He asked to bring you in for an interview. Be ready the day after tomorrow, alright? Just wanted to tell you that.'

Pleased at hearing the news, I immediately said, 'Thanks, Ranjan. How can I repay this great favour you've done me?'

He too replied quickly, 'I didn't do much. What's the use of knowing each other if I can't even do something as simple as this?' He continued on his way.

'Relationships are certainly odd,' I thought. 'Sometimes strangers leave a big impression on your heart; give you happiness. At other times, those whom you call your own break your heart; leave you with nothing but tears.'

As these thoughts filled my mind, my mobile phone rang suddenly. It was Aahil calling.

'Ali, where are you?'

'I'm strolling around Wellesley Street.'

'Are you on your way back?' he asked.

'I am on my way,' I replied.

'What's the matter? Is everything okay?' I asked as soon as I got home.

'It's okay – it is what it is,' Ali trailed off.

After a bit, Ali sighed deeply and said, 'I feel that my

son has become very distant – doesn't listen to what I say; doesn't come home on time. His eyes look listless all the time – like he is intoxicated. He doesn't leave his room when at home; doesn't show any interest when I ask him to visit with relatives. I don't know what to do. I am very worried, Ali.'

'Don't worry so much. He has grown up. He goes to university. If he desires a little bit of solitude, what's so wrong with that? You should try to be more understanding,' I tried to advise Aahil.

'More understanding? He doesn't respect me as one should a father! How can I think that is normal? Is this how a relationship between a father and a son should be? Always on his mobile and laptop! Like an addict to devices. He doesn't bother to converse with our friends! Has he ever spoken properly with you – except for once or twice? He refuses to go to the mosque,' he lamented. 'What conclusions am I to draw from all this? What has happened to kids today?'

'You are worrying without cause. He is learning new technology. What's the harm in that? What young person doesn't use technology today? Let alone young people, you and I have become device addicts! Okay, maybe he doesn't want to go to the mosque anymore, but you should consider this quite normal. Perhaps these things don't mean much to him in his life. Just because we prioritize some things doesn't mean that our children will take up the same things.' It was Hasita who tried to give advice this time.

'Don't pipe up in the middle! Our son has lost his way because of you. I am never going to forgive you for this. Remember that!' Aahil was unreasonably angry at Hasita.

'I came to this country for Baber. For his future. But I also wish for him to not forget his family values. Is it wrong to want that? I feel everything is slipping away from my hands. We didn't have much time when he was growing up. Today, he is grown up. Now he doesn't have time for us,' Aahil moaned.

'He will be alright. Just give him some time. Talk to him; try to understand him,' I tried to comfort him as I gave him advice.

'It's too late now, Ali. My son is no longer close to me. We weren't serious about how he was growing up. Now he doesn't take anything we say seriously.' Aahil's voice sounded tired.

I tried to reason with him, 'Why do you put so much pressure on your son? What has he done wrong? Maybe he likes being alone. Perhaps he is burdened by others' company. Maybe he won't live for your benefit. He might not live for his children's benefit either. Maybe he will live just for himself. Maybe that's what he's learned from Canadian society. His priorities seem to be different.'

'I thought your advice would give me some peace of mind. But...' Aahil trailed off.

'I can't lie to my friend just to make him feel better, Aahil,' I shot back.

Both of us were quiet after that. I felt uncomfortable.

Finally, Hasita broke the ice – 'Have you had any

developments regarding a job? It won't take time for your money to run out if you stay idle for long.'

'I have been called for an interview at a department store,' I replied.

'I am glad,' she said. 'Make sure you are well prepared,' she advised. 'And have you found an apartment yet?'

'I have made inquiries. Don't worry, I am going to move out soon,' I said with a smile.

I could understand Aahil's pain – I was sad for him. He found it difficult to accept his son's indifference. However, there was not much I could do. He wasn't in a state of mind to be able to understand Baber. Baber didn't seem gracious towards his father either. Father and son were living in their own separate worlds – with their own private pains. These two represented two different generations. They grew up in different circumstances – had differing attitudes towards life. These different points of view were waging a jihad against each other under the same roof.

Days went by. Aahil and Hasita were busy with their jobs. I moved to my own flat. We spoke to each other less frequently after that. The distance between us grew.

As it is, friendship is a temporary proposition – a temporary emotion; something that changes numerous times over a lifetime. Friendship is an experience that is born with each new relationship.

But there was a different reason for the growing distance

between Aahil and I. I had brought only a limited amount of money from Pakistan. My pockets were getting lighter. I hadn't secured a job yet. He was worried I would ask him for money. That was the sole reason for the deterioration of our relationship – money.

In the end, it is wealth that defines our identity in the modern world. In this age, wealth is greater than knowledge or wisdom; greater than hard work and perseverance; than civilization and culture. It is greater than your parents, your siblings, friends, neighbourhood, society or your nation. Extreme greed for money has become the world's universal maxim today. This greed has resulted in humanity's difficulties today.

It has spread like a pandemic – a disease that has no treatment. I was beginning to see a similarity between Canadian and Pakistani societies. They had both become enslaved to money. Scholars say that every age invents some medium in order to rule over the world. Tools to hunt animals were such a medium in prehistoric times, and religion in the medieval times. Modern age has money. Information technology and biotech are the mediums for the future.

However, I wasn't unhappy with Aahil's conduct. I prefer clarity in life. I am incapable of deception, and I don't believe in opportunistic relationships. I like to move forward whatever the circumstance. I was offended by Aahil's behaviour, but it wasn't my sole responsibility to maintain the relationship. After all, life doesn't stop in the absence of one relationship. Of course, it is painful when a childhood friend becomes estranged. However, I decided to carry on down my own path. Unable to get a job related to civil engineering, I took on a basic job with the help of Ranjan – as a simple employee at a department store. During the night shift to top it off.

Love

It wasn't easy for me to work the night shift. I had no prior experience of working such hours. Yet somehow I managed to get myself accustomed to it. My job started with training in how to make various kinds of breadstuffs. Ranjan Khatiwada was my supervisor and gave me my training.

Ranjan had been living in Toronto with his wife and son since 1998. He wasn't very old – he must have been around forty-five. He was slender with noticeable lines on both his cheeks. He wasn't the type to relax while others did all the work. All the employees liked him. He treated everyone like family. He was especially skilled at training new hires. Our relationship deepened. His heart was as pure as the driven snow – totally guileless. He couldn't keep anything hidden.

One winter night he told me, 'I don't like the Canadian education system, Ali!'

'But the education system here is renowned all over the world. Some universities here are world class,' I countered.

'Canadians are good at teaching,' he quickly responded, 'but they don't like learning.'

'Can you explain what you mean by that? What do they need to learn?'

'Perhaps the education system in other countries is not as good as it is here, but it also isn't as bad as they think it is. I got a master's degree from Tribhuvan University in Nepal. Then, I taught students at the same level for thirteen years. Yet they tell me that I have to do my bachelor's again!'

'Because they have a different grading system here,' I explained.

'I would have agreed if they'd asked me to improve my language. Especially French and English, because my grasp of both is not as strong as I'd like. But they tell me that I have to improve the content, that the education I had back home isn't enough – that it's not up to their standards. What about all the education beyond university? All that experience? They don't value it at all. Ridiculous!'

'Is it really that surprising?' I asked. 'Isn't some type of benchmark necessary to determine whether someone is qualified for a bachelor's program or a master's program?'

'I am tired, Ali. I won't go to these universities any more. I will work hard, and just make a lot of money. One day my son will go to a university. I have already studied as far as I wanted. And I already earned all the respect I wanted back in Nepal. Now I don't desire anything else.

'Why did you leave Nepal if you are so unhappy here?' I asked.

'In search of happiness. But happiness is a mirage. I am only beginning to understand that now.'

I could understand Ranjan's pain. Yet I could give him nothing besides my sympathy. My own situation was analogous to his – I was compelled to work at a department store even though I was a civil engineer. Many like me come to this country to learn new skills in their respective fields. Yet we utilize these skills nowhere but in local department stores and watering holes.

Most immigrant stories are similar to each other. A majority leave their homes because they are exhausted by the political and economic instability in their countries. Some leave to secure the future of their children. Others leave because they are denied employment opportunities. Some leave for education while others believe immigration a progress in itself. They don't have great big desires either – good schools for their children; good environment for raising them. And opportunities for good jobs.

In today's world, these simple desires are believed to be connected to human rights. Unfortunately, the countries of their birth confine these rights to the pages they are written on. At least large democratic countries have realized these rights – implemented them in the regular citizen's life. Yet even the majority of them limit themselves to basic rights.

I wonder – 'How much progress has democracy managed to achieve? Where do men at the centre of this system stand today? How fulfilled are they? How deficient? How easy and natural are they? How artificial? Are they whole? Or fragmented? Are they vibrant? Or lifeless?

Ranjan was just a representative. Of a system that has failed everywhere – in his own country as well as in Canada. Ranjan used to say – 'People have gained rights in Nepal. But those rights are only for the powerful. For the vast majority, those rights are confined to the books.' Canada had a bit of freedom. Yet in differing quantities for residents of different classes. White Canadians who were born and raised in Canada enjoyed more rights than new immigrants or the Asians who were born there – not as a matter of law but as a matter of practice.

The people who had migrated to Canada two centuries ago were in the first class. Those who had arrived more recently were in the second class. In the first class were those who had come to Canada to escape economic hardship; in the second were those who were brought to Canada to rapidly advance its economy. Ranjan belonged Canada's second class of permanent residents.

He had exchanged his inner satisfaction for the struggles in Canada. It was a transaction of his heart for the economic advancement of his family. Therefore, he endured his share of hardship. In today's global democratic system, we all have our own share of 'private islands'. And modern men are cursed to live alone on their own 'island,' embracing their own struggles, yet hiding those struggles from the world – constantly being beaten down. Ranjan had survived in that manner, by keeping himself busy day and night. I too followed his example. And in order to improve my own self-confidence, I started working during the day.

It was when working the day shift that I made a new friend, Riya. There were many others who worked at the store, but Riya caught my attention swiftly. Why wouldn't I be attracted to Riya? I found her quite mysterious. She must have been about twenty-five. She exuded a powerful radiance. She was dusky, cool like the morning dew. Slender, lissom, with long graceful fingers. Her eyes lined with kohl and pupils as if they were swimming in celestial wine. Extremely seductive – an unparalleled beauty. My ego had lost its being before that beauty. She was always narrating her story – not in words but in the various ways she presented herself.

Actually we are all stories. Different stories. Some long, some short. Some deep, some superficial. Some lifeless, some vibrant.

She seemed to view others with a bit of indifference. I'd never seen her speak with any of my colleagues. Perhaps she was spellbound by the arrogance of her own beauty. Everyone at the store was constantly trying to draw her attention. I too wanted to strike up a conversation with her. But how? What if she totally ignored me when I went up to talk to her?

Then, as if by providence, the store manager appeared before me and said, 'Ali, you will be getting your training from Riya.'

'Riya, you need to get Ali trained. You have a week to

get him ready. There are few reliable people to work the night shift. He has the ability; he just needs a good trainer. You are the most suitable person for that.'

'I'll try,' said Riya and then turning to me right away she said, 'Ali, please take a look at this guide booklet.'

'What is this?' I asked.

'Read it first. Then you will understand on your own.' I found her tone a bit brusque. It disappointed me. I felt it pierce my heart. I was unnerved, but tried to get on top of the situation by heeding her.

'Oh, this lists all the rules that need to be followed in order to sell cigarettes,' I said.

'Yes. It is essential that all new employees learn this. It's not simple – selling cigarettes in Canada. You have to follow the government rules. As per the rules, you can't sell cigarettes to anyone below nineteen years of age. And you don't need permission from anybody to ask for and check the identification of young customers. If you sell cigarettes to the under-aged, you might have to pay a big fine. The store might even lose its licence to sell cigarettes,' she explained.

I pretended to listen to her attentively. I didn't have any particular interest in the rules governing the sale of cigarettes. I just wanted an excuse to get close to her. 'What other things carry a fine in Canada?' I asked sarcastically.

'You pay a huge fine here if you are unable to make money. If you have money, everything is okay. If you don't, then there's nothing. You have to pay fines if you can't pay your rent or phone bills on time,' she replied without hesitation. 'And another thing. If you want to work at this store for any length of time, memorize the price codes for all the items in this store. I don't want to have to help you forever.'

'Yes, I can imagine. You seem like you are unwilling to do many things in life,' I said a bit brazenly.

'I'm also unwilling to talk about useless things during work hours,' she responded without missing a beat.

I'd managed to speak to Riya but I was angry at myself for being so impudent with her. It was my fault. I wanted to get to know everything about her in the very first meeting – learn her entire story. Yet my conduct pushed her away from me.

However, people who work in the same place have to speak to each other at one time or another, despite any reluctance. After all, she was my trainer. Over time, Riya and I started talking to each other. Slowly, the distance between us grew smaller. We started to get to know each other. But how well, it was hard to say. As it is, even a lifetime is insufficient to really get to know another person; we were but merely spending together what little time we stole while rushing about our jobs. During those early days, I only learned that she had come from India.

One day, when there were no customers at the store, I asked, 'How many days of the week do you work, Riya?'

'Five days – I don't work on the weekends,' she said.

'There's a nice restaurant on Gerard Street that serves Pakistani, Indian and Bangladeshi food. Have you been there?'

'No, I haven't.'

'Why don't we go one day?' I suggested.

'I've known you for only a short time!' She looked at me in surprise.

'Haven't we become friends? And there isn't much that's important to know about me. I have been an average person all my life,' I said.

'There is something important to know about every person – each person is special. And every person hides something from the world,' she said in a mocking tone.

So, I started telling Riya about myself at every opportunity, whether at lunch or when there were no customers at the store. I didn't care whether she wanted to know anything about me or not. I described in detail how I got to Canada, losing my self-respect in front of her. Yet I was pleased. Because Riya seemed to be paying attention to me. She was a bit more relaxed with me after learning about my family life. Perhaps knowing that I had a wife and a daughter made her feel comfortable.

Then one day she agreed to go out to lunch with me.

'Why did she agree to the lunch?' I was certain I didn't have the qualities that attract people. 'Was she really interested in me? And what was the nature of that interest?' I lost myself in thought.

My curiosity knew no bounds. There was a certain excitement in my heart. I started getting ready to meet her. I spent a long time in front of the mirror that day. I took out the brown suit I had brought from Pakistan. I hadn't worn that suit in Canada prior to that. Suitably attired, I reached the Alibaba restaurant on Gerard Street exactly at 12:45 pm. We had agreed to meet at one o'clock.

I waited for Riya. She arrived on time. I couldn't believe my eyes when I saw her in front of me. Wrapped from top to bottom in a deep red one-piece dress Riya had not just caught my attention but that of everyone present. It was as if her seductive body was attempting to jump out of her dress. My eyes stayed on her body for a long time, seeking something in her. I was trying to catch a glimpse of the real Riya who resided under that body.

Realizing that she might get uncomfortable by my staring, I said quietly, 'Please sit down. Why are you still standing?'

'Thank you,' she said and sat down in the chair in front of me.

'What do you want to eat?' I asked.

'It's been a long time since I've had chicken biryani. I'll have that today,' she replied.

I signalled the waiter over and said, 'One chicken and one mutton biryani.'

'Would you like something to drink, sir?' the waiter asked.

'A mango juice for me. And for madam?' I looked towards Riya.

'An orange juice for me.'

I couldn't wait for the waiter to leave. As soon as he left with our order, I said, 'Red looks really good on you.' She smiled. I also smiled but couldn't flirt with her more than that. I didn't know how. Changing the subject, I asked,

'What brought you to Canada?'

'Money,' she said, 'It was difficult to support the household with my salary.'

'You had a job? And your parents? Who else is in your house?'

'My parents are quite prosperous,' said Riya, 'I worked for my husband and daughter.'

'You are married? And you have a daughter? It's hard to believe. You don't look married. You look so young.'

Getting serious at my reaction, she said, 'I got married right after I finished my bachelor's. I met my husband in college. I was in the first year when I met him. He was in his final year. We used to see each other from time to time because we were in the same department. But those meetings turned into love before we realized it. We decided to get married after I graduated. But my parents didn't like my decision. I tried to convince them but they didn't agree. When everything failed, I married Rohit without their permission. Our daughter was born after a year. My parents still haven't forgiven me, even after the birth of their grand-daughter.'

'Oh, then you live with your husband and daughter here?'

'No, they live in India. My husband had a motorcycle accident – exactly a year after our wedding. Our daughter had just been born. He hasn't been able to walk since then. He was the sole breadwinner of our family – his job had supported us. After he became bedridden, things got really difficult for us. So I left him and my daughter in my in-laws' care and came here. I send a bit of money every month. That has been enough for now.'

Her eyes were moist by the time she finished speaking. I was also finding it quite difficult to keep my composure. I was looking for the right words to say when I blurted out, 'Oh what misfortune! How incredible that you're able to carry such a burden at such a young age. This makes me very sad.'

Wiping the tears off her eyes she said, 'I have become used to it. No need to be sad on my account.'

I couldn't say anything for a while. I didn't have the courage to ask her more about herself and her family.

After a short silence, I asked, 'Where do you live here?'

'In Islington.'

'Oh, that's quite far, isn't it? Especially from where we work. Don't you get tired commuting to work and back?'

'Of course I get tired. But rent is quite cheap in Islington. A person like me, whose main aim is to save money, has to stay a bit far from the centre. I rent a small room there. That room is my whole world in Canada.

'Does someone else live there?'

'No one beside the landlords.'

'I agree. It's better to be alone in a crowded city,' I said.

'People are always alone, Ali,' she said, 'whether they live alone or in a group.'

'Where are you getting these deep thoughts?' I asked her teasingly.

'Experience teaches you everything, Ali.'

Trying to change the subject, I asked, 'What are your

hobbies? What do you like to do in your free time?'

'There isn't much that's interesting. I don't have a particular hobby. In India I used to go to the cinema with my husband, but that seems like a dream now.'

'So what do you do on your days off?'

'Just regular chores. Clean my room, do some shopping, buy groceries. Talk to my husband and daughter on Skype; look at them; think about them. I go to Montreal sometimes.'

'Montreal? Why?'

'I have a cousin there – Nikita. She lives in Montreal with her family. I go and stay with her sometimes.'

Riya described her life in detail. We had finished our food by then. We decided to part soon after that. We both had work the next day. And I had run out of questions by then.

Alone on my way back home, I wondered – 'What must Riya have thought about me?' She probably thought – 'The most boring person I have met until now!' I concluded. But then again, I thought it was no longer important what Riya thought about me. She had agreed to have lunch with me. There was nothing more pleasing to me than that.

When I saw Riya for the first time at the store, I had guessed that she must have gone through quite an upheaval in her life. I thought so because of her tendency to stay aloof from others and be lost in herself. Yet, I could never have imagined that her life was filled with such sorrow. Mother to a small girl, wife to a paralyzed man, struggling alone in Canada so that her family in India could live in some comfort. She had suffered so much pain.

'Do her own personal desires have any value for her?' I wondered. 'Has she ever lived just for herself? As 'Riya,' and not as someone's wife or someone's mother? Is she happy in this country? She'd followed a singular course in Canada; lived only one kind of life – room, work, then back to her room. How could she be happy with such a life? Why is she being denied every kind of happiness in life? What a misfortune?'

'Could I be of some help? But would it be appropriate for me to try? Why not? But has she asked me for any kind of help? What if she thinks of it as an encroachment on her personal life? After all, we've only had one meal together. But no, I don't see why she would think of this as an encroachment on her life. If she didn't want any help from me, then why did she detail her entire life to me? And what harm is there in my helping her? After all, I am a sensitive person. In fact, getting to help her is my right!'

'Men have always considered it their right to encroach upon women's lives. That too in the guise of a protector!'

That night, thoughts of Riya kept running through my mind. At some point, unconsciously, I fell into a deep sleep. In my sleep that voice returned and said, 'Wake up, Ali. You have been asleep for a lifetime. Now wake up.'

The next day, I was at work, but my mind was not on it. I was back on the night shift, after four weeks on the day shift. The manager had arranged my schedule that way. Many of my colleagues didn't like working at night. I also didn't like it, but what could I do? I was obliged. Those who had been working for a long time got preference for the day shift.

It was difficult to work at night in some ways, but it was also easier in other ways. First, you'd be away from the manager's gaze. He came to the store only at seven in the morning. So you'd get to be your own boss. Second, you'd get to meet all kinds of people at night – especially the drunks. While a few of them weren't any good, some were perfectly fine.

Some colleagues who'd worked the night shift at the same store had got good jobs based on the relationships built during those times. But nothing of the sort happened to me. Many had promised, but the promises made while drunk weren't kept. As it is, people are intoxicated for most of their life. Some are intoxicated because they've imbibed alcohol while some others are intoxicated by wealth, power and social status. In the present age, man's conscience is injured. Therefore, he likes to live in deceptive light.

Riya had gone to Montreal on a break from her work. I recalled her telling me about a distant cousin who lived in Montreal. Perhaps she'd gone to stay with that same cousin. We hadn't been able to speak before she'd left. Yet I was continually absorbed in her thoughts. She would incarnate in my mind like a bright luminescence. The thought of her alone would excite me. 'Is she now my only remaining friend?' I asked myself. 'I can't see anyone beside me except her,' I concluded. I waited for her return with great anticipation and impatience.

One day I went to the store to pick up my pay check. I was hoping to run into Riya. And sure enough, she was working. My happiness knew no bounds on seeing her.

'Riya, how are you? When did you come back?' I asked from a distance.

'Only yesterday,' she responded.

'Why didn't you call?'

'I thought I'd just see you here. But you've started working the night shift. I was going to call you today,' she replied. 'But what are you doing here at this time?'

'I came to pick up my pay check. My daughter has sent her birthday wish from Pakistan. She wants an iPad this year. Since her birthday is just next week, I thought I'd buy one and send it on its way.'

'Ah, okay. I will call you after work then,' she said, and went back to work.

I picked up the check and left. I deposited the check at the bank and drew some money from the ATM. After leaving the bank, I was browsing around at a store when Riya's words suddenly started resonating in my head – 'I will call you after work.'

'Yes, she said she'd call me! Then, she too wants to talk to me.' I got excited. I was thinking about her when my phone rang. I answered promptly, 'What's up Riya?'

'I just finished at work. It was very busy today. Did you buy the iPad for your daughter?'

'No, I haven't. I just got some cash out.'

'What are you doing on Saturday? Do you want to go to the cinema?' she asked

'What else do I have to do? I am free. I haven't been to the theatres in Canada yet. It should be fun,' I said.

'Let's go to an evening show,' she suggested. 'And we can go out to dinner afterwards.'

'Of course,' I said.

'Alright then, let's meet on Saturday,' she said and hung up the phone.

'Is this a dream or reality? What is happening to Riya? Why is she giving me such importance?' I couldn't comprehend. But my joy knew no bounds.

That Saturday we met at the theatre located at Yonge and Dundas. Riya had decided to watch a Bollywood film called 'Rishtey'. The film was more than two and a half hours long and completely worthless. It was very difficult for us to sit through the film.

After exiting the theatre, I asked, 'What's happened to films these days? Why are they so bad? Films used to be really good back in the day.'

'Times have changed, Ali. Films today aren't like the ones in the past. Some new movies are extremely good, but others useless. Our fate gave us the useless kind this time.'

'Forget this! I am quite hungry. Let's go get something to eat. Do you want to go to Alibaba and eat biryani again?'

'No, let's go to a pub today; have a few drinks. We will decide on food later.'

'Where do you want to go,' I asked.

'Have you heard of the Imperial Pub?' she asked.

'How would an infrequent drinker like me know of Imperial Pub?'

'I haven't been either. But I've heard a lot about it – that it's a great place; that they have live jazz!' Riya informed me.

'Alight, let's go there then,' I agreed.

We arrived at the pub. It was built in the classical European architectural style; I was charmed the moment I saw it. Groups of all ages – students, middle aged, young – seemed content with drinks in their hands. We went up to a table and sat down.

'What will you have, Ali?'

'A glass of wine is enough for me.'

'What good is one glass going to do? Let's ask for a bottle. We will share it,' said Riya.

'Looks like I'm gonna get drunk tonight,' I said amused.

'I asked you to the pub, so I'll treat you with the bottle,' she said and went and got a bottle of wine and two glasses.

'Do you drink often?' I asked.

'No, I don't. But I feel like it sometimes. It's fun to get intoxicated and forget one's troubles at times. Don't you think so?' she asked.

'I'm not much of a connoisseur. I may have drunk only a handful of times in all my life. That too covertly.'

'I feel like you've done a lot of things in your life in

secret,' she smiled at me mockingly.

'No, Riya, I am not the secretive kind,' I said. 'You tell me. You must have some secrets.' It was my turn to inquire.

'It would have been fun if I had a few. But I don't have any,' she laughed.

'How was your time in Quebec?' I asked changing the subject. 'I've heard that it is a very beautiful place.'

'You've heard correctly. You have to visit Quebec at least once, Ali. It is very beautiful. Both English and French cultures live side by side there. Quietly. Holding on to their own identities. And oh, you have to go to its museums! They reflect the historicity of the city. But I didn't have much fun this time.'

She didn't seem to want to elaborate.

'Why? What happened?' I pressed a bit.

'Why are my relatives so nosy about my affairs?' she said without looking at me. 'I thought I'd spend a nice few days with my cousin, but Nikita exhausted me with her questions! How much do I earn? What do I do with my money? How much do I send home? Why does she need to know all of this?' And that's not all! How many friends do I have in Toronto? Who are they? Do I have to give her an account of everything? Why can't they leave me alone?'

'Because despite being a married woman, you live here alone, Riya,' I said.

'Do married women have to provide a detailed report to their relatives just because they live alone?' she asked. 'Do you think so, Ali?'

'Perhaps they are worried about you,' I said.

'Worried? About me? I haven't heard anything more ridiculous!' she said angrily.

I didn't say anything at first, but then added, 'It's not good to get upset on account of others' reactions, Riya.'

'It would be one thing if others behaved like that, but I can't understand why Nikita would act this way. Why is her mentality like this even after going to such a fancy university?'

'Going to university alone doesn't guarantee anything. What has she specialized in?' I asked.

'I don't know the exact topic, but she is doing a PhD in gender studies. Forget her – she is a distant cousin. Sometimes my own husband and in-laws display the same behaviour; their questions aren't much different from Nikita's. It makes me very upset. I have given up my entire life for them. I endure all this hardship for them – I earn. But they? They can't even trust me! I am tired of everyone. I have no desire for anything anymore, Ali.'

'What are you saying? I don't think your family would send you off to Canada alone if they didn't trust you,' I tried to comfort her. 'Relatives are different. They are always critical of their relations. That's how they are. You should take it in your stride.'

'I have some distant cousins-in-law in Toronto. I don't see them. And they in turn have no desire to see me either. I hear they're unhappy with the work I do. Apparently it's not up to their standards. They're ashamed of calling me their relative,' I confessed in solidarity. 'Now, is there any cure to this kind of illness?' I asked.

'What nonsense! And what do they do?' asked Riya.

'They drive taxis at night. But they lie about it to their families back home,' I said.

'They lie? But why?' Riya asked in surprise.

'They're afraid of losing face.'

'Yet they say your work is embarrassing!' Riya exclaimed. 'What kind of people are these?'

'I don't think it's because of my work that they keep their distance from me, Riya.'

'Then why do they keep their distance?' she asked.

'Because I don't hide the nature of my work from society. Because I can't lie to others like they do. This distance is brought on by my own integrity. It's difficult to lead an honest life. I haven't chosen solitude without reason,' I said with a laugh.

Riya gazed at me without saying anything.

'People like to create false impressions about themselves and live according to that,' I added. 'They create false identities and then strive to earn false recognition for those false identities. These false recognitions aren't built on the foundation of reality. They are built by lying to society, by throwing sand in its eyes. Man leaves no stone unturned to demonstrate that he is in possession of all the markers that society considers ideal. But in reality he doesn't have those qualities. As a result, each person creates two identities for himself. One is the identity based on reality that doesn't have the need for any recognition; the other is the esteemed personality that is replete with fraud.'

'There is a constant conflict between these two aspects in a person's life. Unfortunately, the identity created on false esteem always wins. Because society imbues false esteem with power; grants it legitimacy. Society encourages duplicity. That truth always wins is just a mere impression – a story constructed by society to perpetuate the illusion that life is meaningful; a narrative invented to keep society within bounds; a melody composed to provide meaning to work. Actually, falsehood is stronger in every age. Therefore, every person wants to rule over others; exploit them using various means. Your relatives, husband and in-laws want to similarly control your life and exploit it in the same way my relatives try to do to mine. None of us are ever free, Riya.'

Riya continued to stare at me for a long time and then nodded her head. 'You speak the truth. I agree with you completely.'

'You and I also want to dominate each other,' I added.

She furrowed her brows and looked at me, 'I'm finding you a lot different from what I initially thought of you.'

'And what did you think of me, Riya?'

'An old man, lost in himself, always looking for opportunities to speak with pretty women,' she giggled.

'You are right,' I also laughed. 'I am a man lost in myself. But I'm not chasing any woman, okay?' Then I added with some playfulness, 'Don't believe for a second that you are beautiful. You aren't all that pretty.'

She didn't say anything else. We had finished two bottles of wine by the time we were done talking. I hadn't imbibed like that in a very long time. We were both drunk.

'I had a lot of fun today, Ali. Thanks for keeping me company. I feel rejuvenated – like my stresses have been washed away,' she started to talk again.

'It's I who must thank you,' I said. 'I don't have anyone here. Your company has made me very happy – you can't even imagine. It's very difficult to find trustworthy people these days. I am fortunate in that respect.'

To tell the truth, her words had assuaged my ego. A person like me, who had been lonely for a long time, had found the company of a beautiful young woman. Riya had appeared before me as a living breathing godsend. My heart was dancing for joy. She had revealed the depths of her nature and understanding that evening. I was even more attracted to her. I felt that we had surrendered ourselves to each other. Yet the submission felt like victory. Like we'd fulfilled each other's desires. At least I was feeling that way. I could neither move nor say anything. Riya too seemed frozen in place – speechless.

'Are you still not hungry?' I asked after a while, breaking the silence.

'Of course I am – we haven't eaten anything,' she replied.

'The biryani place is probably closed now. The only other option is my flat. If you're comfortable with it, we can go look in my kitchen. It's also getting too late for you to get back. You can consider my studio flat your own home,' I suggested.

'If I were uncomfortable, I wouldn't spend all this time with you, Ali! But tell me, do you have more wine at home?' she asked.

'I have one bottle,' I said. 'I bought it when I moved into my flat. I got it with the intention of celebrating the start of my new life in Toronto. But it remains unopened. Perhaps it too was waiting for the right guest.'

We started drinking as soon as we got home. In fact, we drank even more quickly. We were quite intoxicated by the time we finished that bottle.

'I'd never imagined that I'd be drinking wine with you in my flat, Riya. I have been attracted to you from the moment I first saw you at the store. I have long dreamed about this day,' I blurted out.

'Really?'

'Really. I was alone in Toronto. I was looking for a friend with whom I can freely be exactly who I am – without any disguise; without any mask.'

'But there are others at the store. Why did you choose me?' she asked.

'Don't ask me that. Because I don't know. Does a crazed heart need a reason? I find you genuine and guileless. Perhaps I wanted to become whole through you. I have wanted you from the day I saw you.'

I had never thought I would be expressing my feelings for her in this way. Words spilled out, exposing my heart – the poor heart I had hidden from everyone. I was getting embarrassed.

I became quiet.

'I am drinking wine with a man who is my father's age. That too in his flat,' she said breaking her silence. 'I had never imagined that such a day would come in my life.'

'So what pushed you towards me, Riya?' I asked.

'I don't know. I guess we do a lot of things in life without knowing why.'

'Then how does it feel drinking wine with a man who is your father's age?'

'Perhaps the same as a middle-aged father might feel drinking wine with a woman his daughter's age. I don't think our experiences can be that different.'

'Your words are as beautiful as you are, Riya! I am enticed by your fragrant hair that reaches all the way down your back,' the words cascaded out of my mouth.

She became shy and didn't say anything. We just stared at each other for a long time. All of a sudden, some powerful force took me under its control and pushed me towards Riya. I moved close and kissed her on her lips. I don't know where I got the courage to do that. She didn't react for a while. Then, all of a sudden, she started to cry.

'What's wrong, Riya? Why are you crying?' I asked immediately.

'What will my husband say if he finds out about us?' she said softly.

I drew back. I didn't know what to say. 'You are not deceiving your husband, Riya. You are just being truthful to yourself.' The ludicrous words escaped my mouth.

'I hate you, Ali,' she said, 'It's impossible to let you go.' And with that she embraced me. 'Please don't leave me.'

'I won't, Riya. We will be together for the rest of our lives.'

After that, we surrendered ourselves to each other completely.

The following morning wasn't a normal morning for me. Riya's presence made me feel that my life had been adorned in a hundred different ways. She was still asleep. I made breakfast while she slept. She woke up after a while. She got up and stared at me intently. I returned her gaze. It felt as if she was uncomfortable being there with me.

'Last night was a mistake, Ali,' she said as she continued to look at me. 'We are both married and have families.'

'We will talk about this later, okay?' I said.

'But how could I....' she started stuttering.

'What's done is done, Riya. We have plenty of time to talk about this. Don't be too hard on yourself,' I tried to comfort her. 'We both love our families. We understand our responsibilities towards them. But we also have our individual lives. We have certain primal needs. The beautiful time we spent with each other yesterday is our personal treasure. There's no need for anyone else to know about it.'

'But we are not just individuals, Ali. We are also part of families,' Riya argued.

'Family is an institution created by society in order to arrange society in a particular framework. However, a person's life cannot be constrained within predetermined limits. We are made of different emotions. We can neither totally understand these emotions nor control them completely. It's man's nature to sometimes swim along with these emotions, because man is helpless in their face.

This is what happened to us. We aren't about to abandon our families. We have to keep them safe. But we also have to make space within ourselves to cherish those moments that we spent together. We have to lead both those lives.'

'How can we lead double lives? Isn't that deceit? A contradiction?' she questioned.

Her questions made me uncomfortable. I remained quiet for a while. I didn't know how to respond.

After a moment's silence, I looked into her eyes and said, 'Look, Riya, everyone in this world leads a double life. I do and so do you. We all do. One life operates physically, the other spiritually. One runs according to your brain, the other according to wisdom. One runs according to your mind, the other according to your conscience. Whether we articulate that for ourselves or acknowledge it in front of others is a different matter.'

'Would you love me the same if your wife and daughter were here?' Riya asked.

'I didn't get close to you because they aren't here with me in Canada. I became close to you because of the emptiness I feel within me. This emptiness was with me when I was back in Pakistan and is present here in Canada as well. An emptiness that keeps me lonely even when I am in a crowd.'

The first few days weren't easy for Riya. For a while she felt uncomfortable about us. As time passed, it became simpler for us to embrace each other and make love. We experienced worlds in our respective small rooms – sometimes in hers and at other times in mine. I used to buy her presents; take her to restaurants and the cinema. She also bought me presents and surprised me with plans to visit different places during our time off.

I forgot that my wife Zara and daughter Ayesha were also a part of this world. I had completely lost myself in Riya. My world at that time began with Riya and ended with her. But we kept our love a secret – a secret buried deep within us. Years went by in this manner, and we wished for things to carry on in the same way. But for ages, society has been extinguishing love. Our love too was unable to continue evading the prying eyes of society.

Despite our best efforts, the Pakistani eyes at 240 Wellesley Street East started questioning us. Colleagues at the store started questioning me. In the beginning, I tried to fend off those questions. I didn't take any of it seriously until Aahil called me one day and asked me about it.

He called me early one morning. 'Ali, how have you been?'

'I am well, how are you? How are Hasita and your son?'

'They're fine. They're both busy in their own little worlds. You also seem to be quite busy these days?' Aahil asked pointedly.

'I have been quite busy at work, Aahil.'

He was quiet for a moment. I didn't add anything either.

Suddenly he broke the silence and asked teasingly, 'I

hear that some new friends have entered your life. Is it true?'

I was speechless for a moment. I understood that he was hinting about Riya.

'What are you trying to say?' I was a bit flustered.

Taking advantage of our old friendship, he teased, 'You are skilled at finding lovers even at this age, aren't you?'

'What are you talking about, Aahil? Don't people make new friends when moving to new places for work? Didn't you make new friends?' I asked.

'Yes I did. But I didn't have any one special like Riya. I still have a few friends at 240 Wellesley Street East,' he pointed out.

'Aahil, she is just my colleague. How could you think such a thing?' I tried to regain my composure.

'It's not me who thinks such a thing. People are talking about you.'

'People seem to have a lot of free time to pry into others' lives.'

'You are still a casanova, Ali,' Aahil laughed at the other end of the phone.

'Don't talk such nonsense with me, Aahil,' I shouted into the phone.

'Please come over to the house sometime. We will talk in leisure.'

'Sure, I will come as soon as I have some free time.' I hung up the phone.

Aahil finding out about Riya became a new headache for me. He was still in touch with many others in Pakistan.

'What if Zara finds out about all this through them?' I was worried. I needed Riya, therefore, it was difficult to let her go. But I also didn't want the world to find out about our relationship. I wanted to keep Riya close to me forever. But away from the prying eyes of others.

My wife Zara was a reality endorsed by society. Riya was a reality established in my heart. Zara was the truth as defined by society; Riya was a truth forbidden by it. I came to the conclusion that I had to abandon my heart in order to live in society. 'Don't worry. You are not alone,' I tried to comfort myself despite the sorrow I felt at having to leave the one person I truly loved. 'Everyone here lives without a heart.'

There was one question that troubled me – 'If Riya finds out that I don't want to see her any more, how will she react? What will she think of me?'

Then again I thought, 'She will understand if I explained myself properly.'

'Will she be willing to let go of me if she knows of my reasons?' I despaired again.

I had only one option that allowed me to save myself from society's ridicule while not having to immediately break up with Riya, which was to go back to the schedule of working the night shift where I wouldn't have to see Riya every day. And, that's exactly what I decided to do.

Separation

I returned to the night shift – a nine-hour shift. After working all night, I used to get back to the flat, eat breakfast, and sleep all day. With this schedule, I barely had time to see Riya. She used to call me a lot but I always made some excuse or the other.

Work too had seen some changes. Ranjan worked the night shift as always, but a new associate, William, had recently joined as his assistant. William was a white man who was born and raised in Canada. He was about forty-five years old. Stocky and muscular with a full round face and big bushy eyebrows, he was fond of food and loved to make conversation. We became fast friends.

I used to ask him about Canadian society, especially about the social, political and cultural changes in the last few decades. I also tried to find out his personal views on the policies regarding immigrants that Canada had put into law. He shared his opinions freely and easily. William, in turn, would question me in detail about my family and Pakistan. Our friendship deepened.

Days went by. It was 27 December 2007. I saw on the news that Benazir Bhutto, the Pakistani leader, had been assassinated. I was stunned. I cast my mind back to my student activism during the 1980s. I thought about her family. I thought about her father. I thought about her. True to her name, she really was unlike anyone else. I believed that Pakistan would never have someone like her again. And with a heavy heart, I offered my prayers to her.

That's not to say that she wasn't allegedly embroiled in various corruption scandals. But her will to bring change to Pakistan was indomitable. Before she was assassinated, she had lost her father as well as two younger brothers. They were all killed by the dictatorship in Pakistan. The Bhutto family had made a huge contribution to modernize Pakistan. Therefore, her assassination was no trivial matter. Like me, numerous Pakistanis would have been enraged by her assassination. I was afraid there was going to be unrest in Pakistan. I called Zara immediately.

'Zara, are you all alright? What's the situation there?'

'We are all okay. Why are you in such a panic?'

'Benazir's assassination could bring about clashes. Please be careful,' I said.

Zara's response was no different from the usual. She said curtly, 'Nothing like that is going to happen. It's natural to be nervous when you're far away. But don't worry. We are okay. And Ayesha is my responsibility. Not yours.'

'Goodness, Zara! Why do you act like this on the phone? What is the meaning of repeatedly saying that Ayesha is only your responsibility? What are you trying to say? Why don't you ever understand that I worry about you two constantly. That's why I call you so often. But I see I made an error in calling you right now!' I hung up the phone in anger.

Disappointed and feeling disrespected, I could think of no one besides Riya at that moment – the same Riya whom I had been ignoring for some time now.

'How can I call her now? What will she say? What will she think?' I was disturbed by these questions in my head. But then I thought, 'Why shouldn't I call her? After all, I can say I was busy with work.'

I called her. 'Riya, how are you doing?'

'I am okay. How are you? You remembered me after such a long time today. I called so many times, but you never answered.'

'What can I say? I get really tired after working all night. I sleep all day. You know how it is with night shifts. But forget about these things. I am off from work this weekend. Are you busy with something then?' I asked.

'I don't have much going on. You know how it is with me. I want to make something delicious this Saturday. Why don't you come?'

Riya said exactly what I was hoping she would say. She invited me to her place. She saved me from embarrassment. 'Okay. I'll come,' I said quickly. I thought about Riya only when I needed some personal support – to quench my physical and psychological thirst.

On Saturday evening, I bought a bottle of wine and headed towards Riya's place. We would be seeing each other after a very long time.

We hugged as soon as we saw each other without uttering a word. We didn't want to let each other go from that embrace – as if repaying the loan of love with interest. Freeing herself from my grasp, she said lovingly, 'I've made *nihari* for you.'

'Why did you go through all that trouble? Do you really love me so much? You know how much I love *nihari*,' I said.

'That's why I made it,' she smiled. Then quickly turning towards me, she said, 'You don't pay much attention to me these days. Why are you ignoring me? Can't you see how much pain that causes me?'

'Why are you asking me this ridiculous question? It's nothing like that. It's just that I am really busy at work.' I tried to sidestep her questions.

'You only get in touch when you need me. And when you don't, you can't be bothered less. Do you think I am a puppet to be treated however you wish?' she asked, her voice rising with the questions. 'Don't think for a second that I don't see through your behaviour.'

Her questions distressed me a lot. They accused me of using her. Remaining composed, I tried to mollify her, 'Riya, why are you asking these hurtful questions? It's not at all like that. Please believe me.'

'Yes, you keep saying that,' she replied, 'but your actions prove different. You are no longer the same Ali I used to love.'

'Stop all this nonsense,' I yelled, suddenly losing my composure. 'I already have a wife. I have no interest in taking another!'

'What have you turned me into, Ali?' she said disappointedly.

'You're not a child,' I said, my voice was still raised. 'How can I make you do anything at all? You did it all on your own. Only you can be responsible for your decisions.'

'You have become very cruel these days, Ali,' she said dejected. 'I never expected this.'

I remained quiet for a while before saying, 'I think it's best we went our separate ways. It's not right for us to compromise our families for our personal pleasure.'

Riya didn't say anything for a long time. She seemed stunned by my words. Then suddenly she exploded in anger, 'Personal pleasure? Is that what this is? Was our intimacy just for personal pleasure? And where is this sudden concern for your family coming from? Weren't you completely fed up with your wife Zara?'

I couldn't say anything.

'But you are right,' she added. 'We should never have begun this relationship. I knew that in the end, this would happen. That's why I used to ignore everyone. That's why I tried to keep my distance from you in the beginning. Yet, somehow you became an important part of my life. I couldn't dam my feelings for you. I knew that we both had families. But… I made a big mistake loving you. Now I will go back to India. To be with my family. Lately, I let myself forget the truth about my life. And your reality isn't much different from mine either. The only difference is that you are a man, and I, a woman. You will be forgiven for our relationship. But a great many questions will be asked of me. Regardless, it's best we part. But is it necessary to do it this brutally?'

True to her female heart, Riya was treating me with love even as we were separating.

'Please believe me when I say that I don't want to hurt you. People everywhere have been talking about our relationship. What would happen if our families found out about it? Can you imagine that?' I asked with compassion.

'You are worried only about yourself, Ali, not about me. You have been concerned only with yourself all your life. Why didn't you discuss the matter with me even once before making such a big decision? You got close to me when it suited you, and when it didn't, you deserted me. Is this how things work in the world of men? Is this how your love works?

'I accept that I made a mistake in not discussing things with you, Riya, but please consider this – who in their right mind would leave a woman who loves the way you do? I'm afraid there's nothing I can say that will make you understand. Please forgive me,' I said with great sadness in my heart, 'I can't continue with our relationship.'

'It's alright, Ali. I don't expect you to either.'

We kept looking at each other without saying anything.

I felt as if my own silence was pressing down on me. I had never felt so helpless in all my life. As I tried to compose myself, the words just came out, 'I think I'll leave now.'

'Why don't you eat before you leave?' she said

'I am not worthy of your love, Riya.' And with that I left her flat with a heavy heart. She didn't try to stop me either.

I never attempted to get in touch with her after that day. I didn't feel like seeing her either. I would smile and wave at her when I saw her at work occasionally; she would smile back. Initially, a few colleagues at work did ask if everything was okay between the two of us. But after we stopped seeing each other completely, that meddling also dissipated.

In truth, without Riya, I was living an empty life. I loved her with all my heart. How could someone not love someone as authentic and guileless as she? She lived deep in my consciousness. But I never expressed that to her. There's a limit to how much a married man can express his love for his lover; I was bound within that perimeter.

With Riya, I had managed to unveil a version of myself that I had hidden deep within me – a version that I had hidden away from the outside world. It was a self that contained both positive and negative aspects. And Riya was acquainted with both of those. I had loved her, but also deserted her. I was never able to forgive myself for leaving her. As it is, self-criticism is never easy for anyone.

There was only one way for me to free myself of that feeling. It was to keep myself extremely busy at work. And that's what I did. I started working six nights a week. Yet I was unable to liberate myself from thinking about Riya. I hadn't liked Canada to begin with; I really didn't want to stay there after breaking up with Riya. The cold in Canada started to distress me even more. I concluded that I had to leave Canada. Without even consulting Zara, I decided to return to Pakistan. After that, I started working day and night – to earn some money to take back with me. I had no other priority except for work.

Ranjan had been a big help to me at work from the very beginning. Now William was proving very helpful as well. Because we had become quite close, I once asked him a personal question, 'William, are you married?'

'You need a close friend first in order to get married, Ali. I haven't found one yet,' he replied with a laugh. 'I can't even afford a girlfriend, how am I to get married?' he added.

'I don't get it. What do you mean you cannot afford a girlfriend?' I asked.

'Girlfriends are very expensive these days, Ali. You need lots of time to maintain a relationship. You need money. You have to buy her drinks, take her to restaurants, and periodically buy her presents. How can someone like me who makes eleven dollars an hour afford a girlfriend? Who's going to pay for food and rent?'

'Then will you stay unmarried all your life?' I asked.

'It's possible. I don't know. But I can neither afford a girlfriend nor a wife in these circumstances. Our standard of living has gone down. Everything has become more expensive. But our income has been stuck at the same place,' he said. 'Just look at me,' he added, 'I have completely become an automaton – I spend all my time trying to make money; then I spend it all on rent and food. Where am I going to find the money to spend on family, friends or relatives?'

'Why don't you take a higher paying job then? You must be able to find a good job?' I asked.

'Where are the jobs? There are no jobs in this market. I have a bachelor's degree in photography. But technology has consigned my profession into the wastebasket.' he said.

'I thought that only immigrants found it difficult to get jobs, but I was wrong. I guess there are many Canadians like you as well,' I said with sympathy.

'It's not just the immigrants who are having a hard time. Immigration has indeed made it more difficult to find jobs; there is more competition, and that's the truth. But it is also true that there are very few jobs all around. Whether it's immigrants or natives – everybody is facing the same difficulties. Times have changed. And with changing times people have become displaced. This is the age of machines, Ali,' he explained.

'Just look at me,' he went on, 'I was born and raised here in Canada. Yet I am working here alongside immigrants like you. But what's bad about that? It's not like this place is beneath me. All work is the same. It's nice if you can find a high paying job. But whether or not you get such a job depends on what you've studied. If you have a degree in information technology or related to finance, then your chances of getting jobs are better; things are more difficult in other fields.'

He then asked, 'Why did you decide to come to Canada, Ali?'

'Our society is rife with myriad problems, William. Political instability, poverty, lack of employment opportunities are just some examples. No one happily leaves their home and family to go to a strange country without good reason.'

'You're right. But why don't people want to change their situation? Why do they just complain that this or that thing is wrong? Why is everyone running away from their reality? I'm not saying that people shouldn't come to Canada. But what I don't understand is how this culture of flight from third world countries has come to take root?' he asked.

William's questions made me uneasy. I was afraid he had plainly deemed me to be a runaway from my country. I didn't have an immediate answer for him. I was a bit flustered, but I composed myself, thought for a moment, and replied, 'I don't know much but they say that all of this started with the advent of globalization. Scholars agree that ideas, capital, as well as human resources move swiftly from one country to another. Perhaps that's why people from other countries have arrived here. Maybe it looks like flight from your point of view but on closer inspection, it seems that these people are being buffeted by these global processes.' Then I added, 'It's easy to ask these questions from where you stand. But it's quite difficult to live with these questions day after day.'

'I understand, Ali. It's not easy. But we all have to start somewhere, don't we? Just look at us. Canada wasn't made in a day. Our ancestors went through a lot of hardships for us. Perhaps Pakistan today isn't where you'd like it to be. But if people with skills like you return home and intervene, then perhaps the situation can change. If you don't decide to take up action on behalf of your descendants, then nothing will happen. Your generation has to make some sacrifices. Your sacrifices today will ensure that some future Ali does not have to leave his family.'

'Common people like us are always surrounded by problems,' I said. 'What can the powerless like me do against the political and social systems that are adept at oppressing us?'

'You can always do something, Ali. You can help bring about small changes. Don't focus on big changes. You don't have enough time for them. Actually, change is an illusion. There's no such thing. On the surface, everything seems to be changing. At certain times, social and political systems seem to change. Weather changes. A child grows up to be old, then dies. But look deeply and you will see that nothing changes. Everything and every life moves in a particular manner; on a particular path; in the same direction – towards death. Our destination is fixed. Time's direction is fixed. Where do you see actual change? Why are you so determined to make change?'

'If change isn't possible, then why intervene at all,

William?' I asked. 'We could just as well do nothing. We might as well stop living.'

'What alternative do we have besides living? Therefore, it's important to do something while we are alive. We have to do our work. But we shouldn't be too fixated on thinking whether or not that work will bring change. Despite cutting edge advances in science, we have been unable to understand all the mysteries of life. Nor can we understand the mysteries of death. At a certain point, your body stops working – life is extinguished from the muscles. The bones in your body don't move on their own. Biology and anatomy don't explain the source of life. Have you ever thought – 'what exactly is within us that gives this collection of muscle and bones the form of life? What is this source of life? Where is this source? How does it enter a person's body? And where does it go when it leaves the body? Social and natural sciences consider life to be mere probability. So why all this helplessness over a life that is merely a probability? Thus, why give up on life just for fear of instability and death? There is only one thing that is under our control. And that is our personal decision making. And that's personal – it's right there in the phrase! It's something that you can figure out for yourself. But even that feels like only a partial truth because many of our personal decisions are influenced by external factors. However, we can ignore those influences and call our decisions personal, and we can either continue living the way we do or decide on how else we are going to live our lives. Ali, if I were in your shoes, I would not stay one more minute in Canada, so far away from my family.'

'You are right, William. I am someone who prefers solitude. I thought that I'd get that here in Canada – away from the daily bickering with my wife. That's why I came here. But I have wanted to return from the very moment I arrived. I think I'd prefer that very bickering. I am also encouraged by your suggestion. I am going to return soon. I've grown tired. Now I want to spend my remaining years with my family.'

'That's great news, Ali! You have my best wishes.'

'Thank you, William. I am trying to save some money. I will probably work for another month or two. Then I shall return to Pakistan. Thanks again for your advice.'

Time seemed to move faster. I didn't notice the two months go by. Perhaps because it was nearly time to go home, my heart was overjoyed. I had never experienced such joy before. It was as if I was getting reunited with myself; going back to my roots. I had been waiting for this moment for the last seven years. It was like being freed from a long detention. I was eager to return to Pakistan.

I felt I should see Riya before I left. Without thinking too much about it, I called her. 'Riya, how are you doing?'

'I am doing okay, Ali. You called after a long time – what's new with you?' she said in one breath.

'I am also doing well, Riya. I called to see if I could meet you.'

'You want to meet? Didn't you just want to get away from me recently?' she asked sarcastically.

'I have to tell you something important, Riya,' I said with a lot of feeling.

'Okay. I want to hear what you have to say. Let's get some coffee this Saturday. At Tim Hortons. 4:00 pm?'

'Okay. I will see you at four there,' I said and hung up.

My heart was a whirlwind of emotions on Saturday morning. I was particularly mournful because I would never be able to see Riya after I returned to Pakistan. That day, even the wind felt like it was moving very gently, as if it was softly singing into my ears the songs of our love – the songs of our separation.

I steeled my heart and headed towards Tim Hortons. I thought about our relationship the whole way there. I wanted to forget everything that had happened between us. I wanted to forget the fight we had – even our love. I wanted to forget the way I had behaved with her; though, I neither regretted the past nor felt ashamed of it. I believed that Riya would forgive me. These thoughts were playing on my mind when I reached the Tim Hortons on King Street West.

The café was close to our work place. She had already arrived when I reached. I approached the table where she was sitting. Unable to utter a single word, I simply stared at her. She too just looked at me. The old formality was back in her look. But her eyes were moist. There was love reflected in those moist eyes. Riya had only love to give, which she gave to everyone. I too got a share of that love.

'I am really happy to see you, Riya,' I said with a tremble in my voice.

'I'm glad to see you too. What are you doing these days? Tell me!'

'Not much. I am going back to Pakistan,' I said promptly. I was in a rush to tell her the news of my return.

'Oh, have a good time then! When are you coming back?' she asked.

'I am not coming back. I will stay there,' I said.

'Forever? But why?' Riya was surprised.

'I am tired of running away from myself, Riya. I have had enough. Yes, things aren't perfect in Pakistan. Zara won't be pleased with my decision either. But I want to spend my remaining years with my family; with my daughter; with friends and relatives. I have earned everything that the common man prioritizes. I'm recognized by a few people. I've saved up a little bit of money. I have a family. I have relatives, and friends. What else do I need? I ran like a madman all these years to earn those things. But that struggle has actually impoverished me. I feel that I am losing my humanity. The course of life has stripped me of my dignity, Riya. 'I want to die like a human being. And to become human, I have to slow down the pace of my life. I have to sit still with myself. In this place, there is nothing but a mad rush for everything. It is a place full of noise – of the screams of everyone scrambling to fulfil their basic needs. Canadian society can give me nothing but this.'

'Can it not give you anything?' Riya asked. 'What else

do you need besides that? Isn't the entirety of our life's struggle to secure a home, a car, the future of our children, health and education? Isn't that the purpose of our birth? Millions around the world are constantly struggling to achieve the very same. And the people who already have them, to keep them secure. And some, to save as much as they can. This accumulation is a never ending process. And every person is a participant in this process. This is the natural fate of man. It starts with our very birth. And you want freedom from this process. We can't be free of it until our death.'

'You are right, Riya. I seek to free myself from that very cycle. I am searching for something else. I want to break free from the prison of desires. After all, I can't take those desires with me when I die,' I replied. As I spoke, I felt an unusual tremble in my voice.

'Not a single person in the world takes anything with them when they die. Why are you trying to be different from everyone else? Why are you trying to be special?' Riya asked.

'I am not trying to be special, Riya. Life and death should be different from each other. What's important in life should not be important in death. I spent too much time adorning my life. Now it's time for me to prepare for death. I have reached that age. Therefore, my priorities have changed,' I said.

Then I added, 'Please think carefully. Look at me. Look at yourself. Look around us. We are but nothing. This nothing has been embellished. What kind of embellishment is this that manifests nothingness as existence? At the same time, there are elements of ego in each beautiful life that lead the ego towards nothingness.'

'What in the world are you talking about?' Riya exclaimed totally confused.

'Forget these things, Riya. I came here to apologize to you. I behaved poorly with you. I used you. I also betrayed my wife and daughter. I used everyone I met in life for my own advantage. I have had enough of that. I want to put an end to this process. I won't see you again,' I said in a single breath. I felt lighter.

'We all get used. Sometimes knowingly and at other times, unwittingly; sometimes in love, and sometimes in deceit. Women have been living like this for ages. By wringing the life out of our internal emotions; by making it colourless – like a robot. We do possess emotions, but for ages, these emotions have been suppressed by society. Therefore, we find it natural to be used,' said Riya.

'But don't worry, Ali,' she added, 'men usually don't admit to their mistakes like you did; I consider myself lucky in that regard. And I don't believe that you used me – it was my decision to be with you. I spent some of the best moments of my life with you, and I will cherish those moments – in my heart. Only you and I will truly know the depth of our love.'

'I learnt a lot from you. You loved me at a time when I needed that love the most. You breathed new life into me, helped me experience life anew. You made me understand that each relationship is unique. I created a new identity for myself in your presence – an identity that isn't tied to the existence of my husband or daughter – an independent identity. I wasn't independent; you helped me be that,' Riya said softly.

'Perhaps this is what they mean when they talk about a woman's love. You loved me despite my selfishness. It wasn't right how I acted with you. My love was transactional. I will always live with that guilt. Yet, you honour me in this way with your words. I am humbled by your love and recognition. You are exceptional. Truly exceptional,' I said. 'When I was with you, I loved you. But even when I wasn't with you, I always thought about you. And I prayed that you'd be able to return to India soon,' I added.

'I too am not blameless, Ali. My love wasn't selfless either. I sowed the seeds of your love on the grave of my husband's love. I embraced you by renouncing Rohit. Love itself is not discriminating. Different people use love differently, and make unbiased love prejudiced – desecrate it. But I am happy for you today. You are returning home. Go home with a happy heart.' Her voice was full of love and sympathy for me.

'Thank you, Riya. You endured a difficult person like me,' I said and then asked her, 'What is your plan? When will you return to India?'

'You have to pay a price to sustain relationships in this day and age, Ali. For now, it's enough to send money instead of spending it on a plane ticket. My family needs money right now, not me. When they start to feel that they need me, I will return. Then I won't come back to Canada.'

'Alright, Riya, I have to get going. I'll take your leave. All the best to you for your future. Flowers will bloom in your life as well. Don't worry.'

Riya didn't say anything. Just as I was about to leave, she asked me in a heavy voice, 'Did you ever love me for real?'

Her question distressed me a great deal. Suddenly, my eyes teared up; I couldn't stop the flow of tears. 'You will always remain an extremely beautiful part of my life, Riya,' I said with sadness, 'a part that didn't get a chance to bloom. My secret. Therefore, also my identity. People hide their true identities somewhere deep within themselves. You are such an identity within me. You are the only one who will be with me on my deathbed. Only my final breath will extinguish your memory, because letting you go is possible only with my death.'

'Will we ever meet again?' she asked yet again.

'Not in person. But that is not necessary, because our love isn't tied to any condition. Nor is it bound by any limits,' I said.

As I was saying goodbye, Riya said, 'Your love provides me with contentment. I will continue to preserve that love while I live. Please live well and in happiness. That's all I wish for you.'

It wasn't easy to say goodbye to Riya. But I also didn't find it too difficult to leave. I thought that it was my good fortune to meet Riya in Canada – her presence addressed the emptiness in my life. And my presence, in her life – even if just for a fraction of all the moments that made up her entire life – was a beautiful story that made my own existence meaningful. Our fates had made our meeting meaningful. We had each addressed the other's needs. But after those needs were met, we had gone our separate ways. Perhaps all relationships are like that. They remain intact as long as they mean something – as long as they fulfil some need.

I wanted to see everyone including Aahil, Hasita, Ranjan and William before I returned to Pakistan. But it wasn't possible to see everyone. Each one of them had, in one way or another, contributed to the meaning of my being – the meaning of my existence – my life. Some loved me, others helped me. Some behaved harshly while others were disappointed. Not everyone is the same. I could never have a very good relationship with Hasita. Aahil maintained a normal friendship. I never had any problems with Ranjan and William. Yet, each one had helped me prosper, playing their respective roles. I had to fulfil mine. I didn't have complaints of any kind against anybody.

I called everyone to say goodbye. Aahil wasn't happy with my decision. Ranjan and William were. Everyone had their own opinions about the decision I had taken. I listened to each one of them. I thanked them – for being an important part of my life. I was especially grateful to Aahil. I also thanked Hasita for allowing me to stay at their home during my early days. Hasita advised me to reconsider my decision. She curtly asked me, 'So you've decided to go back to that pit, haven't you?'

'Yes, Hasita, that crumbling pit is my home. It's the same place where my and your ancestors lived their lives – where they struggled – where they took their last breaths. And millions continue to struggle in that same pit in order to realize their dreams,' I said.

'I don't see any kind of future for Pakistan,' she said.

'The possibility of light is found only where there is a constant darkness, Hasita.'

'So you have decided to gamble with your own and your family's life,' she continued.

'Hasita, we live but once. And even that one life is uncertain. Why live it on all fours?'

She understood that I wasn't going to change my decision. 'When are you leaving?' she asked.

'At the end of this month.'

I decided to return to Pakistan on 15 March 2008. I hadn't told Zara and Ayesha about my arrival – I wanted to surprise them. Once again, I was going to be amongst family, relatives and friends. My happiness knew no bounds. I was already lost in dreams about Lahore. I had already started catching the scent of its soil around me. I was already swaying from head to toe to the songs of the famous Amjad Sabri. After so many years away, even the thought of returning to your motherland makes you emotional.

'How am I going to react when I see my daughter Ayesha after such a long time?' I wondered. Technology has eased modern life. While in Canada, I used to talk to my daughter via Skype. But I was meeting her in person after a long time. 'How would they react? Will Zara be happy to see me? She must have changed quite a bit! She had toiled hard for so many years to keep my family together. She looked after my younger brother Akib like a mother would. How different must Lahore have become? The university I went to, the place I used to work at, my friends, relatives!' These thoughts kept playing in my mind; I reminisced about it all.

I arrived home at around two on a Saturday afternoon. I assumed everyone would be home since it was the weekend. But I only saw Akib – he was the only one home.

'Akib, how are you my brother?' I asked.

'Brother!' He promptly gave me a big hug. 'What a happy moment!'

'How's your health brother?' I asked.

'I am well. I take my medication on time. And I listen to *bhabhi* (sister-in-law) as well as Ayesha.'

'You were always a good boy,' I said.

'I didn't know you were coming today. Bhabhi didn't say anything about your arrival,' he said.

'I came without telling anyone, my brother. Even your sister-in-law and niece don't know about this. But where are they?' I asked.

'They've gone out somewhere with Sabir *bhaijaan* (brother). Bhabhi said they would be a bit late,' he answered.

'Sabir? Who is Sabir?' I was curious. 'And have you eaten?'

'I have already eaten, bhaijaan. Bhabhi cooked for me in the morning. Do you not know Sabir bhaijaan? Hasn't bhabhi told you about him? Sabir bhaijaan is bhabhi's friend. He is very kind. He comes to visit often. And he brings candy for Ayesha and presents for me and bhabhi,' Akib detailed.

'Why hasn't Zara told me anything about Sabir?' I wondered. 'Where could they be right now?'

'Where did they go?' I asked Akib. 'Did they tell you?'

'I don't know. Bhabhi didn't say anything. I think they went to the cinemas. They'll be back soon,' he said, then promptly asked, 'Brother, what have you brought for me from Canada?'

'All you can ever think about is getting something from someone! Nothing is ever enough for you, is it, you beggar! You will never let me be at peace. You've made my life a living hell, you lunatic!' I exploded all of a sudden.

'What did I do, my brother? I just asked if you'd brought me a present on returning after all these years. Aren't I allowed to even ask?' Akib became tearful.

I was stunned for a while. What was I saying to my own brother? And why? Where did all this anger come from all of a sudden? I was at a loss.

'I am sorry Akib. I have brought a great many things for you.' I tried to console him.

'Bhabhi also scolds me all the time. I thought I wouldn't have to endure any more scolding after you came back. But you started scolding me the moment you arrived here.' He was still crying.

'Please forgive me, my brother. I will never scold you again.' I hugged him.

Akib held on to me tightly and said, 'It's alright. I will call bhabhi and let her know that you have come home. They will return promptly when they hear that you are home.'

'Oh no, no. There's no need to call. They'll be home soon,' I said.

I dissuaded Akib from calling, but my own mind was running all over the place. 'Who is this Sabir? Why did Zara not tell me anything about him? What kind of relationship do they have? They even go to the cinema together!?' Zara and Ayesha were far from my thoughts. Sabir had taken over my mind.

I became quite agitated thinking about him. I didn't notice time go by. When Zara and company returned home, it was already eight in the evening.

Zara was surprised when she saw me and exclaimed, 'Ayesha, your father has come home!' and turned to me. 'You came without giving us any notice. You are very odd!'

'Would you have been so surprised if I'd sent word? I wanted to see the excitement on your faces,' I said.

'Daddy!' Ayesha gave me a hug quickly.

'Ali, please meet Sabir. I totally forgot to introduce you two,' said Zara.

'Hello Sabir, I am Ali.' I extended my right hand towards him.

'It's nice to meet you,' Sabir extended his hand to meet mine. 'I've wished to meet you for a long time.'

'So, what do you do, Sabir?' I asked.

'Let's save the details for later. You've just been reunited with your family after such a long time. For now, I'll take my leave. If we'd known that you were coming, we wouldn't have gone to the cinema. But I'll go for now. I'll see you again soon.' Sabir got up.

'Wait a while, Sabir. Have some dinner before you go,' I tried to get him to stay.

'We'll have dinner another time, Ali. You must be tired after such a long trip. Please rest for now. We will certainly meet again soon.' Sabir said his goodbyes to Zara and Ayesha and went on his way.

'Alright everyone, get ready for dinner now,' Zara said as soon as Sabir left.

Then she looked at me and said, 'What kind of a stunt is this? You came without telling us! Why did you act so thoughtlessly?' I sat down at the dinner table without responding to Zara.

We were eating dinner as a family for the first time in years. I thanked Allah from the bottom of my heart. Ayesha asked me about Canada so I told everyone about it in detail. I narrated my experiences. I told them about everything except Riya. I also told them about the harsh winters in Canada.

Cutting me off mid-story, and without much warmth, Zara asked, 'So how long are you staying?'

'Forever. I won't go back,' I replied. 'I have had enough

of living alone without you. I won't do it anymore.'

'It's no good operating on emotions alone, Ali. I understand that it was difficult for you to live alone in Canada. But how could you make such a big decision on your own? You didn't ask for my opinion even once! The money you sent was such a big help to us here. You should have stayed there a few more years. You could have returned when we had saved up enough money. We could have all lived happily after that,' Zara elaborated.

'I wouldn't have had any time to spend with our daughter if I'd stayed in Canada any longer. She is going to get married and leave home in a few years. Then when would I spend time with her? Do you still suggest I go back to Canada?' I asked. 'Please have mercy on me, Zara. We can talk about money later. We will think about our income options,' I pleaded with her.

And then I added in anger, 'I feel like you don't want me here. It's as if you don't love me anymore.'

Zara didn't say anything.

'Who is this Sabir?' I asked. 'Are you having an affair with him?'

'You've gone mad, Ali! Have you been taking your medication regularly?' She adroitly avoided answering my question. 'He's just a friend of mine. And I do love you. Now go to sleep. We will talk tomorrow.'

It was the first time I'd seen Zara unable to defend herself. She was a woman who was extremely adept at using logic to deflect blame. She could have easily embarrassed me for making such a grave accusation against her. But she didn't do so. Why?

'Is she really in another relationship?' I wondered.

'That can't be true,' I tried to reassure myself.

'But what if it is true?' then I thought again.

With suspicions running rampant through my mind, I didn't notice when I fell asleep. Once again the shrill voice from deep within me resonated in my sleep, 'Wake up, Ali. You have been asleep for a lifetime. Wake up now.'

Until that particular day, the voice would dissipate after saying those words. I would only listen. But that day, for the first time, I asked it questions – had a dialogue with it.

'Who are you? Why have you haunted me for so many years?' I asked.

'I am you, Ali. Now, wake up. See me. Experience me. It's time. You need me even more now,' the voice said.

'But I do know who I am. I am very tired. Please leave me alone,' I begged off the voice.

'What do you know about yourself, Ali?' the voice pressed on.

'I am a simple Muslim man born in Lahore, Pakistan. I have a wife and a daughter. I also have a younger brother. He needs my special care. I struggled all my life to meet the needs of my family. I spent most of my life trying to achieve peace, stability and security for my family. Now, in the remainder of my life, I want to grow old in the presence of my family members,' I explained.

'Those are just your circumstances. They don't explain who you really are. What is the purpose of your life?' the voice asked again.

'Do I really have to define myself? Is having a purpose in life essential? Why? I don't know any more about myself besides what I just said. I don't really care about anything beyond it either. The purpose of my life is to actually live it. And I think I have lived well,' I said.

'Can a life that has failed to really know itself claim to have lived well?' the voice asked again.

'Alright, please leave at once. I don't want to see you anymore. I don't want to listen to you anymore.' I was getting annoyed.

'I am the one who carries your dreams and ambitions to even greater heights. Recognize me, Ali. I am the cause of your entire existence. I am your ego. Your truth. You have to face me whether you like it or not. The sooner you do it, the better,' the voice said resolutely and then disappeared.

'Tea is ready, Ali. Please get up.' Zara's voice woke me up in the morning.

I had never said anything to Zara about my experience with the voice. I decided to share it with her that day.

'Zara, I've been having this strange recurring dream for a long time. I can't say when exactly it started, but it has been a long time. I haven't told anyone about this, but I want to tell you about it today,' I said.

'What kind of dream, Ali?' Zara asked.

'I hear someone speaking to me in my sleep. It feels like a female voice. It repeatedly says, 'Wake up, Ali. You've been asleep a lifetime.'

Zara let out a giggle as soon as she heard me.

'Wake up for what? A female voice! It must be the long trip. You were very tired yesterday. Or, did you have a lover in Canada? It must have been her voice that's haunting you.' She made fun of me.

I couldn't say anything for a moment. I turned pale. Then composing myself, I said, 'Don't talk such nonsense. I am telling you the truth.'

'Sounds like you've been ensnared in some delusion. You didn't forget to take your medicine last night, did you?' she asked.

'It was pointless telling you about this. There's no connection between that occurrence and my medication!' I said.

'Your medication keeps your behaviour in check, Ali,' she said. Then changing the subject, she added, 'Alright, let it be. Please get up now. I have to get a lot of things done on Sundays. I won't get as much time after I go back to my regular job tomorrow.'

'What regular job?' I asked.

'I have a regular job, Ali! Did you forget?' she asked. 'What about you? What are you going to do? Have you thought anything about it? You're going to have to do something. You are not the kind who can just laze about doing nothing.'

She was being sarcastic, but I ignored it as if I hadn't even heard her.

Days went by. Zara got busy with her work; Ayesha with her studies. I sometimes helped Zara with the housework. It became my daily routine to buy groceries and look after Akib. Zara was surprised to see me help around the house because I wasn't in the habit of doing so before I went to Canada. I had already fulfilled my obligations of meeting all my relatives and old friends. I started wandering the alleys of Lahore in my free time.

I felt refreshed by the memories of childhood spent in these alleys. From time to time, I also thought about my mother and father. I even visited my old university a few times. Memories from my days on campus would cascade into my mind.

It had been two months since I'd returned from Toronto. I hadn't yet decided what I was going to do for income. Sometimes I thought about making small investments in the businesses of my friends. Then again, I thought I should do something related to agriculture. But I hadn't been able to settle on an option. Zara was getting angrier at my indecision; she started to put some pressure on me.

She would periodically advise me to utilize the experience I had gained working in Canada. 'Why don't you open a small store?' she asked once.

I thought it was a good suggestion. But then I wondered, 'What would my relatives and friends say?'

Six months passed in this way. I neither looked for a job nor started a project during this time. It wasn't that I had no plans, it's just that I was taking my time. Perhaps because I had spent such a long time working in Canada. I was also getting older. So I was in no hurry myself.

One day, I returned home after seeing some old friends. It was a bit late. Zara and Ayesha weren't home. Akib informed me that they had gone out and were eating out as well. Zara hadn't mentioned anything to me. It got to be eleven at night but they didn't return. I called Zara many times on her mobile phone but she didn't pick up. I asked Akib again if his sister in-law had left any specific message. But he told me that she hadn't.

I called Zara's parents and asked about her and Ayesha. They hadn't gone to Zara's parents' either. They advised me not to worry; that they would be back soon. But my heart was getting very restless. I remembered the last argument I had with Zara. She had been really angry with me.

'I can't even keep my own wife happy. I am a pathetic husband,' I berated myself.

Hours passed. But they did not return. Unable to sleep, I paced my room all night. Morning dawned. Suddenly, my eyes fell on an envelope placed on a chair beside the dressing table. Written clearly on the envelope were the words: For Ali. Zara had left a letter for me. I tore open the envelope and read the letter:

> Dear Ali,
>
> You must be surprised to find this letter. And you must also be distressed by our not returning home. But please don't worry about us. We are safe. We are going abroad. We are leaving you and Pakistan forever. We are going with Sabir. Do you remember him? He'd come home with us on the

very day you returned from Canada? I introduced him to you as my friend. Do you remember? But I never told you how much of an old friend or what kind of a friend he was. I want to tell you today.

I have known Sabir for the last twenty-three years. We were in college together. He was three years ahead of me. When my mother first came to me with a proposal of marriage with you, I refused. I repeatedly protested the decision with my mother. I begged and pleaded because no one – you, I or Sabir was going to be happy with it. But no one listened to me.

At a time when no one dared to raise their head and speak up in front of their parents, I had clearly communicated my position. You can probably imagine how deep my love for Sabir was based on the courage I showed at that time. My affection for him remains undiminished even to this day.

Your family and mine had fixed our marriage while we were still young. You know very well that no one listens to daughters in our country. No one listened to me either. I had to submit to my family's decision.

Ali, our wedding took place long after your mother's death. You were only twelve when your mother passed away. Your father raised you and Akib with great difficulty. You may have forgotten how your mother died. Your mother suffered from schizophrenia. She committed suicide.

The remnants of that schizophrenia have endured in you and Akib to this day. Akib's is a bit more extreme; he babbles on his own a lot. The medication that you take regularly keeps your behaviour normal. Yet, sometimes this illness overpowers you. The self-absorbed behaviour that you periodically display is an example of this. We both know this to be true.

Ali, people say that life is a collection of our choices. But I don't feel this reflects the truth. I didn't choose you. I am not saying this because you suffer from schizophrenia. I made a mistake, which was to fall in love – with Sabir. My love for Sabir blossomed even more after you left for Canada. I actually pressured you to go to Canada because of my relationship with Sabir.

But your inner self didn't truly reject my proposal either. You always chose your dreams. The dreams that were woven by your disease called schizophrenia. You have been living with your own delusions. That's why from time to time you like solitude. Delusion is an illness – an illness you suffer from. Therefore, you left us and went to Canada – in search of answers for those important questions about your life that your delusions had created. You always wanted to find yourself; tried to separate yourself from the material aspects of life. You created a world for yourself. And it had no place in it for Ayesha and me. I don't know if the path you chose was right or wrong – I don't understand things that are beyond the material – but I always respected your decision. I always made space for your feelings because I felt that you had no identity beyond these things. But did you ever think about my identity? Forget my individuality, you made fun of every thought I put forward.

You were neither able to become an intimate part of my life, nor did you allow me or our daughter to become an intimate part of yours. Marriage doesn't mean living in one place and dispersing in all directions; it means coming together from separate places and merging into a single unit. Yet this merging does not mean that one needs to completely dissolve one's personality and identity. I can say without a doubt that we are both responsible for the failure of our marriage.

You became a responsible father, husband and elder brother, but you were never able to become a loving father, husband or elder brother. Our structures, values and social systems compelled us to remain together; we ourselves didn't do anything to strengthen our marriage. I was always a burden to you; and you to me. We couldn't move our relationship forward on the basis of love, respect and trust. That's why everything between us has ended.

You will face additional difficulties because of my decision. Our relatives will say all kinds of things about you and me. They will mock you. I can only imagine the kind of aspersions that will be cast on me. Everyone will find fault with me. I'll have to live with these accusations for the rest of my life; endure them until I die. But please don't make any rash decisions in anger because of what I've done – you will need to look after Akib in my absence.

Ali, just understand this one simple thing that I have to say. I'm not against you. It's just that I have loved Sabir to this day. I want to spend the rest of my life with him. You gave me an invaluable gift in the form of our daughter.

I have always taught Ayesha to be independent and self-sufficient. I will continue to do so. Sabir and I will not foist our decisions on her.

She will have the freedom to make her own decisions. One more thing – Ayesha has no problem accepting Sabir as a father. He has spent a lot of time with her in your absence, and has been able to win her over. She knows that we are leaving Pakistan. And she's come with us happily of her own accord.

I wanted you to start doing something. I didn't want you to face any financial difficulties in the future. But you haven't started any work yet. I've saved all the money you sent us from Canada in your account. It will ease things for you and Akib. My decision must have shaken you deeply. But believe me, I haven't wished you any ill will. Nor do I wish you ill in the future.

I don't know if what I have done now, at this age, is right or wrong. I also don't know what consequences will come to bear upon us, but for the first time in life, I am taking a path based on my decision. At least once, I want to try and live life according to my own wishes. I am happy because I have managed to liberate myself before death did it for me. Please forgive me for all the pain this has caused you.

Zara.

A volcano erupted inside me as soon as I finished reading the words imprinted on Zara's letter. Tears streamed down my face. A storm that darkened everything raged within me. I couldn't figure out what to say, or do, where to go, and whom to speak to. There was only one place I could go at that moment – to Zara's parents'. I went to them and showed them the letter. They were dumbfounded. With a quivering voice, Zara's father said, 'Zara is no longer our daughter. She is dead to us. What has that mad woman gone and done at this age!? She won't let us die in peace. Son, please forgive us.'

At home, Akib asked where his bhabhi and niece were. I stopped going out of the house. As days went by, more people found out about the situation. Relatives started to call home. They expressed their concern for me. But they also made fun of me behind my back. Neighbours also came calling to express their concern.

But I couldn't tell anyone what was going on inside me. No one would understand anyway. I kept reading the letter Zara had left me again and again. My tears never stopped no matter how many times I read the letter. I was unable to endure her characterization of me as an unloving father. I could understand why Zara left me. But my daughter? 'Did she not love me either?' I asked myself. 'I wasn't even able to secure my own daughter's love,' I cursed myself.

I spent my days thinking about Zara and Ayesha. I wasn't able to pull myself out of the deep sorrow Zara had caused me. But somehow, I started keeping myself busy with routine chores. Looking after myself and Akib became my primary job. During those trying times, I would sometimes remember Riya. In the absence of Zara and Ayesha, I thought about Riya a lot.

'Riya loved me faithfully,' I would think. 'Should

I return to Canada? But who will look after Akib?' As I mulled over these things, I concluded that no one besides Riya loved me. Then again I asked myself, 'Didn't Riya love her husband too? If she'd only loved me and not her husband, then how was Riya different from Zara?'

I stopped thinking altogether.

During that time, I came to learn about Sabir's family. Sabir had inherited a lot of wealth. He had two daughters from his first marriage – about Ayesha's age. He'd given up his family and his inheritance to start a new life with Zara. 'Did he really give up all these things for Zara?' I couldn't wrap my head around it. Zara was not a young woman. She also wasn't so beautiful that someone would renounce everything for her. Maybe that is why they say 'Love defies all reason'.

'Perhaps Sabir's relationship with Zara developed the same way mine with Riya did,' I thought. 'Then there really is no difference between Sabir and me. He was honest towards Zara and betrayed his wife, as I was faithful to Riya and unfaithful to Zara while in Canada. So it's futile for me to try to pin the blame on someone.'

In Canada, I was terrified that I'd remain alone forever; in Pakistan I was afraid that family members and relatives would never leave me alone. But I was wrong. Now, besides Akib, I had no one left. I had become alone once again.

'The concept of family is a myth. No one is your family. Everyone around you is just an individual,' I concluded. 'Individualistic people aren't found only in the west. People everywhere live only for themselves,' I decided.

I'd gone to Canada because I thought it would secure my family's future. Had I really been able to secure my future? Can anyone ever secure their future? It's impossible to secure one's life. I'd neglected the relationships that I had in order to make new relationships in a place where I was a migrant. I'd attempted repeatedly to redefine myself in order to make myself familiar to a new place. I'd put a mask on my personality. I'd tried to become someone I was not. And despite all those changes I'd been unable to keep my life secure.

I had tried repeatedly to become a new person. I never understood that reinvention is a myth. We all live a little bit in the past, present and future. I hadn't been satisfied with what life gave me while in Pakistan. And I'd lost my entire life chasing a better life. To lose your life before actually dying is to die again and again. In that sense I had died multiple times in my life.

Certain beliefs had inspired me. But I'd made those beliefs my values without understanding their complete meaning. I'd never questioned what it meant to believe in something. More specifically, I hadn't questioned my own beliefs. 'How are beliefs constructed? Who constructs them? At what point do they rise? What's their source? To whom do they provide legitimacy? And how legitimate are they themselves?' I'd never asked such questions.

Under Zara's influence, I'd believed in the prevalent concepts of success. Then I had chased the myth of success. But now, I stood on the heap of corpses of successes. After living under the spell of myths for a long time, I was searching for my truth. I only had one truth at that time – my brother, Akib, who needed my love and care. I started focusing on looking after his health. I opened a small shop in order to cover my expenses. My experience working in Canada buttressed my work here.

And so the days went by. Years went by. Lately I had stopped thinking about Zara and Ayesha. Friends, relatives and neighbours had stopped gossiping about my family. Perhaps they too were occupied by the daily issues they faced. I was getting older. It had been seven years since Zara and Ayesha had left me.

People say, 'Time heals all wounds.' That is only partially true. Time doesn't make you forget everything. It just redirects people's attention somewhere else. As time passes, new issues arise in people's lives. The old is dispersed beyond the horizon. Therefore, the pain dissipates a little bit. I had already accepted my new reality. And I was beginning to get used to that new reality.

Emergence

It must have been towards the end of 2014. I arrived home late one evening after wandering the alleys of Lahore. I checked the computer and was surprised to find an email from Zara. I quickly clicked on the link and read the mail:

Dear Ali,

I trust that, by God's will, you and Akib are well and healthy. I am doing well. I do not want to make this long. I just want to let you know that Ayesha is getting married in three months' time. I want to invite you to her wedding. I trust that you, as her father, will come to the wedding. We will wait for you.

It will be difficult for Akib to also make the journey. You can leave him with my parents. I have sent you a ticket along with this email.

Zara

I was overwhelmed by Zara's letter. Like the torrential rain washes away everything before it, Zara and Ayesha's images cast aside all other thoughts in my head. They claimed every part of my consciousness. 'My daughter Ayesha is getting married,' I had an emotional meltdown. 'What kind of man would she have chosen to be her husband?' All kinds of questions suddenly cropped up in my head. Not knowing what to do, say, or think, I ran to Akib to tell him the news. I told him all about Zara's email. Akib couldn't hold back his tears either and asked, 'Will I get to see my niece and sister-in-law again?'

'I don't know, my brother.'

'Well, you should start making preparations to go to Ayesha's wedding without any delay,' he advised.

I nodded my head in agreement. 'This world is a cruel place, Akib – that calls you diseased,' I cried. We hugged each other in silence for a long time. Akib was invaluable to me. The only one who gave me any support during my most trying times was my sick brother who'd been scorned by society.

I forgot all I'd gone through with Zara in the past, and started my preparations to go to the US. Only Ayesha mattered to me. I wanted to see my daughter in her bridal attire. With this anticipation in my heart, I left Akib with Zara's parents and headed to the US. I also made plans to go to Canada to see my old friends before I returned to Pakistan.

I arrived in New York in the third week of March in 2015. Zara had come to pick me up at John F Kennedy

Airport. She smiled when she saw me. I smiled back at her. Neither of us said anything for a while. I was unsure of what to say. I had stopped blaming her even though my resentment towards her hadn't completely disappeared. It was strange seeing her after such a long time. I wanted to shout at her, ask her why she left me. But something stopped me. I don't know what it was.

I broke the silence – 'How are you Zara?' and teased her about her greying hair, 'You've finally started to look your age.'

She laughed mirthlessly and said in an apologetic voice, 'Please forgive me, Ali. Leaving you was my life's gravest mistake.'

'Gravest mistake?' I asked in surprise. 'Didn't you declare that you'd been liberated by the act of leaving me?'

'Let's just say for now that I was wrong,' she replied quickly. Then she fell silent.

We were inside the taxi. Seeing that she was very emotional and unable to speak, I said, 'Let it be, Zara, let's not talk about it right now. What has happened has happened. I have adjusted to the circumstances – grown accustomed. Let's focus on preparations for Ayesha's wedding. Allah willing, we will have plenty of time after the wedding to talk about ourselves. Let's talk about something else. How's the new city? Is everything going well with you here?'

'I am surviving, Ali,' she said.

'You always insisted that Ayesha stay in Pakistan. At least, that's what you said to counter my suggestion that we all go to Canada together. Now look at you, living in America,' I said teasing her.

'I still don't like this country. We were brought here by Sabir. I didn't willingly choose this country. But I had no choice. Now I can't return to Pakistan even if I wanted to,' she said.

'Oh, I totally forgot about Sabir! How is he doing?' I asked.

'He must be okay. We don't live together anymore,' she said in a single breath.

'What are you saying?' I was bewildered.

'It's a long story. I'll tell you later,' she said. 'We're almost home. Ayesha must have already come.'

'Where does our daughter go?' I asked.

'She has to go to work, doesn't she? Do you think you can live here without working? She'd wanted to take the day off to receive you but I said no. I couldn't be sure what you'd say when you saw me; how you'd act. I was afraid that you'd get angry at me in front of her, so I said no,' Zara explained.

'So how did I act?' I asked.

'You have changed a lot, Ali. You've become a different man. I didn't see you get angry,' she said.

'Why would I get angry? At whom? Turns out there's no point in being angry. I've become old. Time and experience brings some maturity. Times have changed for me, Zara. Changing times teach you how to accustom yourself to new circumstances,' I said with a chuckle.

'How is Akib?' Zara asked softly

'He is fine. He takes his medicine regularly and his health seems to have improved from earlier. He also seems to have come to an understanding with his circumstances. He too has changed quite a bit. There's no one to look after us anymore, so we have started to look after each other. But he often asks about you and Ayesha. and remembers you two a lot,' I said.

I fell silent after saying all that. Zara didn't say anything either. When she grew quiet, I started looking out the taxi window. Soon afterwards, our taxi came to a stop in front of a beautiful tall building.

'Is this where you live?' I asked.

'Yes, on the ninth floor.'

We took the elevator to the night floor.

Zara looked at me and said, 'We're home. Let's go inside.'

We entered a three-bedroom flat.

'Ayesha, look who's here!' Zara said in a cheerful voice.

'Daddy!' Ayesha exclaimed and ran to give me a hug. I held her close.

'My daughter has grown so much. Let me just look at you nicely. It's been so long since I laid my eyes on you. I'd hoped to spend a lot of time with you after my long stay in Canada. But that wish didn't come true.' My eyes teared up.

'Daddy, you have grown old,' Ayesha said caressing my cheeks.

'Of course, my love. It's natural that I'm old. After all, I have a grown-up daughter.'

The three of us stared at each other; hugged each other; and cried for a long time.

'I thought about you a lot, daddy,' Ayesha said.

'Then why didn't you call me even once?' I asked.

'I did want to call you, daddy, but mother would stop me. She always said that you'd never forgive us,' Ayesha said crying.

'I have always loved you and will always love you. What fault was it of yours, my child? Why wouldn't I forgive you? I have even forgiven you mother. I love you both immensely.' I hugged both of them and started crying.

'We left you alone at a time when you needed us the most, daddy,' Ayesha said, still crying.

'You didn't leave me alone, my love. You only kept your mother – someone you loved more than me – company. Your mother looked after you better than I did. She was both a mother and a father to you. I too left you and your mother alone and went to Canada, didn't I? Therefore, I started all of this. The fault is mine. Please forgive me, my child.'

Once again all three of us hugged each other and wept for a long time. We stayed up quite late that night – talking about Lahore; reminiscing about the past.

I found Zara quite reflective. I sensed a deep wistfulness permeating her words. She had changed a lot. I was very happy to see that change in her. I was also especially grateful towards her.

Because of Zara's efforts, Ayesha had become a mature young woman; a modern woman who had a deep love for Pakistan; a self-confident young woman who lived in the modern world without losing her heritage. She was a liberated woman who was ready to face any adversity. She had chosen her own husband. Abbas and Ayesha had studied in the same university in the US. Abbas's father worked at a Pakistani diplomatic agency in New York. All the worries I had about Ayesha's future disappeared. Seeing her the way she was made me very content.

Once Ayesha went to sleep, I asked Zara about Sabir.

'After we came here from Lahore, we lived together for about six months. Everything was fine. But one day, all of a sudden, he declared that he couldn't stay with me. I knew Sabir was wealthy. But he was also lascivious. I didn't know this in Pakistan; I learned about it only after arriving here. Even in Pakistan, he had dalliances with several women; was quite adulterous. He just needed an excuse to separate from me. He came home and said all kinds of things. He said he couldn't tolerate me; he couldn't trust me.

'Couldn't trust you? But why? He couldn't trust you even after you gave up your entire life to be with him? What else did you need to do to win his trust?' I asked.

'It was just his excuse. The truth is that it was a mistake for me to leave you, Ali. Sabir said that any woman who was capable of leaving her loving husband for another man could also leave him at any moment,' Zara recalled.

'What an absurd notion! Sabir wasn't just any other man for you. You knew each other for such a long time – loved and respected each other,' I put forth my observation.

'It was only me who was in love. He used me. But the

main thing is that I was wrong, Ali. Turns out life is a labyrinth in that way. A path that you think is correct at one moment proves to be wrong in another.'

Then she added, 'You went through a lot of pain because of me. This fact will haunt me for the rest of my life. We were humiliated because of me. And Sabir's family was destroyed because of me as well. I will never forgive myself for this. I have to live bearing this sin for the rest of my life. I had Ayesha for support until now, but she will go to her husband's home soon. I will be alone then. I will have to live alone with this pain in my heart.'

My heart grew heavy hearing her words. As if on their own, words flew out of my mouth, 'You can come back to Lahore. We can live together again. I can't see you in this condition. Yes, you did make a mistake but in life everyone makes mistakes.'

'Have you forgiven me then?' she asked.

'It's not only a matter of me forgiving you, Zara. I too have made mistakes. I betrayed you. I wanted to tell you about it as soon as I returned from Canada. But I couldn't do it. I thought I would tell you in due time, but you left with Sabir. Come, let's forgive each other,' I said.

'What are you saying? You betrayed me? How?' Zara's eyes were curious.

'Zara, you've given me a small measure of relief. Otherwise, I would have died under the weight of my own guilt. I did the same to you that you did to me. I am beginning to think that in today's world all one person does to another is deceive them,' I said.

'You are making me needlessly curious,' she said.

'Okay, here it is. When I was in Canada, I met a woman named Riya. We used to work together. She'd come to Canada from India. She was also quite a bit younger than me. In the beginning, we were just friends. But without us knowing it, that friendship turned into love. We loved each other from the depths of our hearts.' I told Zara about Riya in detail.

'I want to visit her in Canada once before returning to Lahore,' I expressed my desire.

'I never imagined that you'd fall in love with such a young woman.' Zara was shocked.

'You're right. I also didn't imagine that you'd fall in love with Sabir. But both these facts are the truths of our lives. If I hadn't told you about Riya, you'd have never known about it. We've spent such a long period of our life together, yet we know so little about each other,' I said.

'Zara, we all have our own small stories – in the deep recesses of our heart. People outside don't see these stories; they just see the covers. Each story gives birth to various characters within us – characters in various guises – kind, loving, hateful, jealous, etcetera. These distinct characters come together to create the whole person. Therefore, no one knows another in totality. The same happened between you and me.'

'You're right. But does it mean that people can't live together just because they can't know each other in totality?' Zara asked.

'People can't live alone, Zara. They're born to live in

communities. Yet this communal notion is not meaningful until the members of those communities don't get to know one another completely. We can stay committed towards each other only if we know each other completely. And the process of getting to know each other is possible only when we begin to excavate the layers within us.'

'Without doing that, I cannot know you, nor can you know me. Only by knowing oneself do we begin to recognize the different dimensions within us. Actually, you, I, or anyone else isn't that distinct from each other. We are all made of similar emotions. When we understand the fact that we aren't that different from each other, we start getting closer, not growing apart,' I said.

'Therefore, you, Sabir, Riya and I aren't different from each other. We are all part of the same truth – at varying levels. We look different on the outside. We may have different perspectives on life. But the atoms that build us are the same. We just utilize those atoms to varying degrees. Our conflicts will end when we understand that truth. Therefore, we all have to explore those atoms inside us. That act will bring us to our primal nature. That primal nature is what manifests all existence – in a single form – in a single truth.

'All of us have to make this journey of exploration on our own. This journey has to become our individual experience. Only such an individual journey can develop communalism. Therefore, the journey towards communalism is only possible through the self. Conversely, the journey towards the self is also only possible through communalism because it is only after the legitimacy of communalism ends that a person returns to the self. Therefore, there is no conflict between the self and communalism. The relationship between life and death is exactly the same. Sunrise and sunset, happiness and pain, beginning and end, are therefore the same. They all start and end at the same origin.

'Therefore the origin is important. The essence of our lives is founded upon our origins. And that essence is the primary mystery of life. We always remain remiss in exploring the essential. Science and civilization have achieved countless things. But even they have missed it. You, I, Sabir and Riya, we are all missing this essence from our lives. We must return to it – to our origin. From now on, I will seek out this very origin throughout my life; search for my essence.'

'Ali, I have never seen you like this. You have changed absolutely and totally. How did this change come about?' Zara asked.

'Zara, all my life I chased the things that had bound me; that raised conflict within me. I never paid attention to those things that could liberate me. What I am telling you today is based on my experience and self-reflection,' I answered.

'So, in that sense, life is extremely important because it brings us face to face with uncommon knowledge and experience, isn't it?' Zara asked.

'Life is important in the sense that it tries to establish a new truth before us – "Life is death and death is life.".'

'Ali, I don't fully understand all the things that you are saying today, but I will ponder these things after Ayesha's wedding. I'll try to understand them. But I want to assure you about one thing, that from now on I will always be with you. Whether I return to Lahore or not,' Zara said.

'It's alright, Zara. Take your time. I too don't know which way I'm headed. Self-awareness is not that easy. It's the point that you reach after which you can't be certain of the journey ahead. But nor can you turn back. Because once you reach the state of self-realization, the purpose of life ends,' I said. 'When egolessness becomes reality, ego itself becomes problematic. Absent a material difference between life and death, life runs into trouble. To experience egolessness while still in existence is perhaps the most terrible revenge that a person can take on themselves. It is the great battle that one wages against oneself.'

'Ali, life is such a strange occurrence. I don't know why, but we begin to understand how to live only in the later stages of life. You started examining your life at the age of sixty. We are close to our deaths. I have begun to feel that one needs to feel death at hand in order to understand life,' she said.

Then both of us went silent for a long time. There wasn't anything left to say. Never before had we spoken to each other like this, delving into each strand of life. This was the first time we had confronted our identities so openly. There wasn't any conflict left between Zara and me; as the matter of honest identity never invites any conflict. The profound peace that we felt within us had tethered us; it had shown us the path to our reconciliation. We had surrendered ourselves to each other for the rest of our lives. We were now connected by a bond stronger than marriage.

'Let's go to sleep now, Ali,' said Zara. 'Ayesha's wedding is nigh. We have to start preparations tomorrow. I was just waiting for you. Now we can see through her wedding together. I finally have some peace.'

'Certainly, Zara. We will work together to make sure that our daughter has a great wedding.'

Days went by. I was extremely happy to be near Ayesha and Zara. Finally, the day to send Ayesha off with her husband arrived. It was a very happy occasion for Zara and me. We sent her off. I didn't want to stay in the US much longer because Akib was alone in Pakistan. And because I had got the news that Riya had returned to India, I wasn't too keen on going to Canada either. I decided to return to Pakistan.

'Zara, I will go back to Pakistan now. You know Akib is alone there,' I said asking for Zara's leave.

'Yes, Ali, I am aware. When are we going to meet next?' she asked.

'Whenever you want. When you decide to return to Pakistan. When you want to reconnect with your roots. I will be there,' I said.

'And when will I be able to reconnect with my roots?' she asked.

'Exactly when you reconnect with your own self,' I said, and with that I returned to Pakistan.

Akib was very happy to see me. I had tasted the elixir of new life after seeing Ayesha and Zara. I was exceedingly happy from deep within. Days went by; I got busy with my work.

The Ali who returned from the US was entirely different from the Ali who had returned from Canada. I had now begun to prepare for my death while I was still alive. In that process I had lost my attraction to people and society. It's not that I didn't love people. Zara, Ayesha, Riya, Aahil, Hasita, Ranjan, William and many others still softly and melodiously whispered in my ears, as if saying something. But I started seeing everyone the same way. Women and men, brown or white, people from different class and communities – all looked the same to me. I had stopped seeing any difference between the greed and selflessness, the cruelty and saintliness, or the disappointment and ambition that they displayed.

After returning from America, I was living in a distinct way. My inner voice, the one that always exhorted me to wake up, had disappeared. I was liberated even from my inner voice. I was detached in such a manner that there was no fear in that solitude. It was at this moment that I started to reflect on my self-image.

I had begun to live a reanimated life after already having been alive for sixty years. Finally, I had arrived home – inside the skin that would one day be buried – into an awesome emptiness. Finally, my exile had ended. And, with this event, I had ended up rebelling against the modern age. Because, with it, I had terminated the physical feeling of my ego. Would I have to pay a price to today's civilized age for such a rebellion?

But I wasn't overly worried about it because I lived in a strange time. Materialism was not only ensnared in a complex web of questions and suspicions, but its foundations and monuments were also being dismantled one by one. Human civilization was beginning to be liberated from the illusion that the current education system is the only ultimate truth. The tragedy of materialism was clear to see in everyone's eyes. The promoters of modernity themselves were screaming for help in order to avoid this tragedy. Like a potter's wheel, modernity's journey was approaching its destination. And concluding with it was the age's arrogance that had long oppressed people. I wasn't too worried about how that diminishing arrogance would deal with me.

There was another part that was more important than this. I had internalized my own self – by letting principles from the past blossom in my heart. After that, the past had no separate meaning for me. Therefore, I packed away all my histories somewhere inside me. The present was standing still in silence somewhere; in the throes of birth; as if human evolution was stuck at some point. Lifeless. In search of freedom.

Yet, I was optimistic about the future. A future that was about to be born out of the wombs of disillusionment and lifelessness. I didn't know how much longer I, a person optimistic about such a future, was going to physically survive, but psychically I was already deceased. And along with me, we all were deceased. Because 'I' am the modern zeitgeist that represents us all. Yet even in death there still remained questions – 'Is this my destiny? Is this all our destinies?'

Along with the questions, emotions welled up like tides:

In the catastrophic present,
the fractured man seeks his destiny,
the meaning of his existence,
his breath.
He seeks his life force.
In the present, consumed in flames,
he seeks his remains.
Lifeless today, in anticipation of tomorrow,
he leans on tradition to stay connected to yesterday.
In this killing field called earth,
he seeks his resurrection,
the meaning of his own existence.
He rebels against meaninglessness,
for he exists,
is diffused from time immemorial to the present,
is anchored from the present to the future,
in various forms,
in various feelings,
for history fractured and fragmented him.
He lost his sense of self,
his dignity,
for religion,
for caste,
for community,

for class,
for gender,
for civilization,
for this tenet and that,
for tradition,
for invention,
for the past,
for the present,
for birth, for age.
Today's fractured man seeks his total existence,
seeks his destiny,
his fortune,
his identity,
his destination.
He seeks his total resurrection.
Oppressed since time immemorial,
he seeks his own reconstruction,
seeks his freedom;
man seeks the meaning of his own existence.

These human sentiments have been expressed in the past. But there's no certainty that they will be expressed again tomorrow. Because of the encroachment of information technology and biotechnology upon him, man is either going to forget how to express sentiments or going to express extremely inauthentic sentiments. One thing is certain regardless of the circumstance – the death of the common man – the death of his natural emotions.

I offered my final tribute to the 'modern man' headed

towards disintegration. Perhaps the people from the middle and dark ages had similarly lamented their own disintegration – to welcome the future. I know there is no allure to this lament. Yet, until he is completely disintegrated, he is obligated to express his sentiments. He is cursed to weep at his own funeral; compelled to sing his lament. After all, what more can a person do when faced with the death of his own self-image that was but a construct of his own era? Or can he remake a 'new' self-image for himself?

ACKNOWLEDGEMENTS

My sincere thanks to my parents, Samir Ghimire and Sarita Ghimire for their tremendous support throughout my life. To my wife, Binu Chaulagain for listening to my ideas about the book and giving feedback to the early drafts. To my son, Samvid for helping me re-imagine the world from an entirely different perspective, making me more mature and loving.

I would also like to thank Sushrut Acharya for the hard work that he has put in translating this work. I am thankful to my friend and literary consultant, Atul K Thakur who remained an insider in its making right from the beginning. Extremely thankful to Manisha Koirala, Professor David Lewis, Aditya Jha, Syed Kashif Raza, Atul K Thakur and Farrukh Sohail Goindi for their praise. I am thankful to Renu Kaul Verma and the entire team at Vitasta Publishing—Alisha Verma, Editor Kanagam King, and Designer Somesh Kumar Mishra for their hard work that has gone into the publishing process.

I am indebted to my friends—Sanjeevani Yonzon, Shakil Ghori and Shams Kazmi, without whose support, this work would not have taken the shape it has now.